HOW to be ME

CATH HOWE

HOW
to be
ME

nosy
crow

First published in the UK in 2020 by Nosy Crow Ltd
The Crow's Nest, 14 Baden Place
Crosby Row, London, SE1 1YW

www.nosycrow.com

ISBN: 978 1 78800 597 5

A CIP catalogue record for this book is available from the British Library.

Printed and bound in Great Britain by Clays Ltd, Elcograf S.p.A.
Typeset by Tiger Media

Papers used by Nosy Crow are made from
wood grown in sustainable forests.

MIX
Paper from
responsible sources
FSC® C018072

1 3 5 7 9 10 8 6 4 2

For Adrian

C. H.

xxx

Chapter 1
Hiding

"Lucas!" Dad's voice rose among the chatting and the tinkling glasses. "Lucas, where are you? Sneaking away, I bet."

I froze in the window seat.

"Come on, my man, we're all waiting for you!"

He would find me; it was only a matter of time. I should never have hidden here. I should have slipped out when they were all cheering. I wriggled in the silky shirt and waistcoat, my stomach churning. There was no escape.

Sure enough, the gold curtain swished back.

"Gotcha!" There was my dad all excited in his evening suit. "Look who I found!" he laughed. "Distinction in Grade Six. Isn't that right, Lucas? Gotta brag about it. Come on." His grinning face was flushed from the champagne.

A hundred people stood sparkling and smiling at me underneath the gold lights of the chandeliers. Dad's engagement party. They had just finished toasting the happy couple and watching the cutting of the Cinderella coach cake. "Just give us a few bars of something," Dad called.

I shrank back against the window.

"Don't embarrass me," Dad hissed. "The piano's waiting." He grabbed my arm and I half fell out of the window seat. "Play something. Anything." He gestured over at the gleaming grand piano on its stage.

Everyone was quiet, waiting.

I shook my head.

"What?" Dad said. "I'm not asking you to do a whole Chopin for us. Just a few bars. For goodness' sake!"

He let go of my arm.

"No," I said, and balled my hands into fists. "There's too many people."

"What?"

Talking broke out. A woman laughed. Glasses began clinking.

"Please..." I said.

Dad stepped back with a terrible, furious face.

He swore under his breath. Then he looked away over his shoulder towards where Vanessa stood, smiling in her pink sparkly dress.

"I'm going to bed," I said, and dived into a gap in the crowd. Then I was running away from him, away from all of them: out of the ballroom, down the corridor, slamming my bedroom door. I couldn't stop shaking. I rubbed away the tears, blew my nose and sat down. Music started up again, thumping through the walls. By now they would be dancing. Vanessa had said she wanted to dance and the band had come specially from a famous jazz club.

My cats were curled up on my bed. I scooped Mowgli up and held him close to my chest. Sometimes he just knew to go very still, lying hot against me.

I got ready for bed. It's much easier to sleep when you have a soft cat to hold, even if there is lots of noise.

Chapter 2
The Mouse

The next day, Saturday, I was upstairs in the ballroom. My cats went wild when I trailed party poppers and burst balloons for them to catch. Mowgli is the dark brown sleek one and Tiger the ginger-striped. Around us the cleaners cleared away all the serving trays and the banners and decorations.

"Lukie! Come down!" I heard Dad call.

I hadn't seen him since yesterday; he often cycled round the park with his friend Steve on Saturday mornings, when he wasn't away on business.

"Back in a minute," I told Mowgli and Tiger.

In the playroom Dad was crouched at the table-tennis table, ready to serve, in his black cycling shirt with all its logos. "Come on, I'm going out again in half an hour. And, boy, do I need a shower."

I slipped into position and grabbed my bat.

"So ... great party. We're all a bit wrecked."

He didn't look cross with me about last night; he just looked ... busy. "So, Lukie Loo ... exciting times." He grinned.

I thought of the speech he had made: everyone laughing, clapping at his jokes, all the excited people and the cutting of the huge meringue and cream cake. Dad was going to marry Vanessa and a hundred people had come round to say well done. And I had ruined it. But Dad was still smiling. "Vanessa's going to be your new mum, Lukie. You could at least look a bit more excited about it."

A new mum. I felt a sick jolt inside me. Mum died three years ago. She had been a warm, kind presence. Meeting me from school, staying beside me whenever I was ill. That couldn't be Vanessa. Vanessa was only interested in chatting and giggling and girls' nights out. Vanessa's job was making jackets for dogs!

Dad was examining his paddle. "Well, holidays for some!" he called, all cheery. "Have you made lots of plans?" He whacked the ball.

I hit it back. "Um."

"You're mumbling," he called.

"Sorry."

We played.

Bok ... bok ... bok.

My head ached. I had kept being woken in the night by the music and voices.

Now Dad leaped and dived after the ball. "Are

you meeting up with your friends?"

"Jasper is in the Seychelles. Marcus is on a boat," I said.

Dad's face changed. "Oh, grim. Both away for the whole summer? Mmm. I don't want you drooping around the place. Piano. Grade Seven. Lots to do for that, I'm sure."

"Miss Connor doesn't do lessons in the holidays," I said.

My piano teacher was so old I wondered if, maybe, she just went to sleep for the holidays. But then in my last lesson of the term she'd shocked me, slamming shut the piano lid and making me turn towards her on the stool. "For goodness' sake, have a bit of fun, Lucas," she'd said.

Dad frowned. "Well, you must have some school projects or something? Your posture's all wrong. Bend your knees."

I whooshed the air, missed and scrambled to collect the ball. I served again but the ball flew off the side of the bat and disappeared into the playroom curtains, so I went burrowing to find it.

"Well," Dad said, "the French chap said he's happy to keep you on next term. Keep beavering away at that. I sent you that vocab app."

I thought of my French tutor Christophe, who smelled like old fireplaces, with his sad droopy moustache. "He doesn't like me," I blurted out. "He looks out of the window."

Dad was staring out of the window too, flexing his shoulder. "Buck up. You don't know that," he said.

Another rally: *bok … bok … bok … bok … bok…* I missed again.

I waited for him to tell me off about last night. I pictured his angry red face in front of all those people. I swiped … missed.

"Let's have a break," he said.

I sipped from a glass of water.

Dad threw himself into a chair.

The smile faded. He started making that face, that *I'm going to fix it* face. He's very good at fixing things, like his bike.

"Anyway, anyway, Lucas, here's another thing: you never speak up for yourself. You don't put your hand up in class. Don't mix."

This wasn't about last night. Dad was talking about school, about everything.

"Your form tutor chap…"

"Mr Joseph," I said quietly.

"That's the one." Dad wiped the back of his hand across his mouth. "He says you're generally far too much of a mouse."

I flushed. Was "mouse" the actual word Mr Joseph had said? He must have been watching me, writing things. Maybe asking the other teachers about me too.

Dad sucked from his sports bottle. It hissed as he took long pulls at it. "Mr Joseph said he never gets a peep out of you. And your little scene last night – well, it's obvious. Now it's the holidays we need to sort you out."

I drummed on the chair.

"Don't drum."

I forced my fingers to be still.

Dad's eyes gleamed. "You need something to take you out of yourself." He walloped my knee. "Leave it with me."

✗

An hour later Dad popped his head round the door of my bedroom. "Sorted," he said. "I've enrolled you in a drama club."

"What?" I stared at him.

"A drama club. Four weeks. Local thing. You can walk there every afternoon. Starts Monday.

Keep you busy."

Why hadn't Dad asked me? Why did he never ask me?

"Things to do, people to see," he said. "Am I sweaty or what? Glad that's all sorted." And he was gone.

A drama club. Horrific!

Chapter 3
The Girl
Gets In!

On Monday, in the afternoon, there I was, stuck!

The summer drama club. It was in a building a bit like a scout hut, boiling hot with no fan, which must be against the law. There were twenty children. My school is all boys, but none of them were here, and there were some girls here as well.

First, a weird, leaping drama teacher called Avalon Jones told us to face each other in pairs on the floor. We were going to play a game called Categories, she told us, as soon as we sat down.

"OK, all of you, think of names of rooms in a house. Shout one word each until you run out of ideas."

She put me with a girl in red tights with the feet chopped off and bare feet. Her jacket, with silver stars sewn on, was too small for her. Her short hair – shorter than mine – stood out in places, dark and clumpy.

We both called out all the obvious answers – *kitchen … bedroom … bathroom … toilet…*

The girl shot her answers at me so fast. All around us other pairs kept shouting out rooms. *Conservatory … hall.*

"Cellar." The girl's eyes were round and flashy, like bright blue marbles.

My turn. I must think of an idea. My mind went blank. Then I had it: "Ballroom."

"*What* did you say?" asked the girl. "Can't hear you."

"Ballroom," I said.

She laughed. "A ballroom is *not* a proper room."

"Yes … it is," I said. "Anyway, it's a stupid game. Your turn."

"A ballroom wouldn't be in a *house*, you banana," said the girl. She never blinked. Her finger poked the frayed ends of her tights. "It's meant to be 'in a house'. You're wrong. I win."

"There could be a ballroom," I said firmly. "I've got one anyway."

"Ha ha! You what? Really?" Her bottom lip jutted out as her mouth opened.

"I won," I said. "We have … in fact … got one." My voice had gone wobbly. "We don't use it, though. Hardly ever."

"You are joking, right? You've got a *ballroom*? That's … that's … that's insane!"

Why was she *so* loud? The nearest boy stopped calling to his partner, his head on one side.

My heart beat fast, enough for a heart attack.

Avalon Jones clapped. "OK, everyone, listening please. Next category, colours. Go!"

"*Red ... blue ... orange ... green...*" chimed out around me.

The girl just sat staring at me. The air got hotter. The floor smelled sour, like school changing rooms. The smell of people's feet.

"So, you've *really* got a ballroom?" the girl said.

I drummed on the floor. "Leave me alone." Then: "Yellow."

"But you have?" She stretched out a leg, flexing, hunkering down on her elbows. Why didn't she stay still?

"Blue," I said. "It's colours now."

"Where do you *live*?" she said, like, *Is it on the moon?*

"Near ... near here," I said. My home, Gladstone House, overlooked the town green. Something twisted in my insides. "You're supposed to be saying colours."

"I can't," she said. "I'm thinking."

"Right, everyone, stop!" called Avalon.

"I win, in fact," I said. But the words were small and far away.

"Who cares about winning?" said the girl. "It's

a warm-up. It's just to make us talk. And I'm too excited!"

This girl had found a door in me and broken in. I shouldn't have to be with her. And, anyway, her feet were dirty. My head pounded. These people were weird.

Dad's drama club was terrible.

I got away from the girl, but I still had to wander around as if I was busy. I noticed an old piano right at the end of the hut. Probably out of tune. I wished I could play it, though.

We had to pretend to be on board a ship. Avalon would tap us on the shoulder and ask us what we were doing. I was panicking inside. What if she tapped me?

I worked out she picked on people who looked at her, so I kept my head down. I would be seasick on the ship, throwing up over the side, I decided. Really ill.

She tapped someone. "I'm watching dolphins," they said.

"Great!" Avalon clapped and her wide sleeves flapped.

The red tights girl leaped on a chair. "I'm climbing the rigging!" she shouted.

Another girl called, "Come on to the deck, Keely!'

Keely. That was red tights girl's name.

She shouldn't climb on that chair. Avalon would tell her off.

She was on tiptoes now, her hand shielding her eyes. 'If there's attackers, we need to see them coming. There's a dark boat on the horizon."

"Great, Keely." Avalon didn't care about the chair. She just smiled. What an odd teacher, not a proper teacher at all.

"OK, everyone. FREEZE!" Avalon said.

Some people became like wobbly scarecrows. I wasn't moving anyway.

"Fab! I love this, guys."

She counted down and we came back to life. The dark boat was much nearer, and it was definitely an enemy.

We didn't have to read anything. No one *ever* put their hand up.

I liked it when the pirates arrived. I didn't say I wanted to be one. But half the group came snarling on to the deck, leaping and threatening. Vanessa said you should breathe out and count if you felt stressed, so I went one … two … three …

four under my breath.

I wondered, would a seasick person still be seasick, even if pirates did come on a ship? Yes, they would, I decided. So, I stayed behind the chair by the window and fiddled with the rusty metal arm, propping it open, wider ... closed. When the attackers rushed in I made up a tune for them in my head. Nobody came near me. They left me alone and tied up everyone else. I wanted to shout, "Look, I survived! I was throwing up over the side. Ta-da!" But no one noticed me. And then the afternoon was over, and everyone was wandering around chatting and Avalon started packing up. So I came out from behind the chair.

A crowd of adults was waiting outside. The big chatting group of kids split into twos and threes, hugging and laughing with the grown-ups.

Our new au pair, Irena, was sitting on the wall. She pulled off her headphones and stood up. She was taller than Eva, the last au pair, with short dark hair. "Where is your water bottle?" she asked.

I went back to get it. The door swung in my face as Keely smashed past. She did a tiny smile, her big blue eyes drilling into me for a second. Instantly I thought about that Categories game and a horrid squirming feeling twisted in my guts. I stood screwing and unscrewing my water bottle until she had definitely disappeared out of sight.

Chapter 4
Cats

On the way home to Gladstone House I walked in front of Irena. It was still baking hot, even though it was nearly evening.

"Your club was good?" Irena asked. But she looked down at her phone again; I don't think she was very interested.

Eva, the last au pair, was kind. She stayed with us for three years. She used to eat a lot of biscuits. She liked little flat ones with raisins in, and she knew which biscuits I liked. Now I felt sad. What was she doing now? Was she looking after someone else?

I pulled out my phone. One message:

Piano practice, French vocabulary, one hour only on screens, super busy, Dad

We didn't have far to walk. The Green is in the centre of town, and people sit out on it or play cricket in the summer. But this summer the grass had dried up. Office workers sat under trees, chatting on benches.

"Wait," Irena kept calling. "Loocas!"

Eva had called me "Loookassse" with a sort of hiss at the end. I liked it. Loookassse. Names are funny. Vanessa, Dad's girlfriend, was "Van" to Dad. And sometimes "little Van Van". "Did you miss me, little Van Van?" Sometimes I was "the boy". "Where's the boy now?" Other times, when Dad was in a good mood, I was "Lukie". It was "Well done, Lukie" if I got a good school report. Vanessa called me "Loo Loo" once. Now she was more careful.

I nipped between the parked cars. Irena caught up with me by the gates, fumbling with her key fob, but I had already pressed mine. I marched ahead of her up the drive, past our fountain of some leaping dolphins. Dad only turns it on at weekends.

It was cooler in the house. In the hall Irena said, "I'll make you food. Do you ... want a drink?"

I flung my rucksack on the floor. "No!"

She looked puzzled. "Your dad said you are hungry."

I hugged the banister. "I'm not."

Her lips bit together and a frown came on her round face. "Bad boy."

She shook her head and disappeared down the corridor to the kitchen.

I sprinted two at a time Olympic-style up the wide staircase and flung open the double doors, calling, "Come to me, cats! Mowgli ...

Tiger. I'm home!"

The huge space opened up, with its gleaming wood floor and arched windows. My ballroom.

My cats raced across the floor to meet me. They snaked round my legs. I bent down and scooped them both up, one on each shoulder. They weren't allowed outside; they were indoor cats. They could go anywhere except the third floor because Dad said their fur made him sneeze. Mowgli had little flecks of rusty colour in the corners of his gold eyes. Tiger's eyes were bright green, like aliens'.

There were three chandeliers in my ballroom. The middle one was the fanciest, the Avalanche, with white crystals dropping down, like snow falling.

Tiger jumped out of my arms the way he always did. But Mowgli just snuggled there on my shoulder. I stood under the lowest point of the Avalanche with Mowgli resting across my chest. "Don't wriggle. Listen to your breathing," I told him.

I hated that drama club. How could I stop going? I stared up into the crystals, my eyes half closed while slices of light leaped and glinted.

Maybe a chandelier would fall on me instead.

The sleek, shiny grand piano stood at the end of the ballroom on a small stage. I gently put Mowgli down. My little polishing cloth was inside the stool. I stroked down from the high notes. *Tinkle tuddle-um bom.*

I did my piano practice: scales and the pieces for my exams. "You're such a musical boy," my teacher, Miss Connor, said. "Practise every day, twice a day, and you'll see results."

I ran back to the ballroom doors and peeped out to be one hundred per cent sure that there was no one anywhere near, then I crossed the ballroom again and scooped up Mowgli to sit beside me on the stool. The whole ballroom was hushed.

I put my hands gently down on the keys, closed my eyes and felt the proper music arrive. My fingers found new tunes from somewhere inside me. This is how it always was. Today my music was called "Blue Marble Eyes", and it made me quake and shudder. I was on the pirate boat in a storm. The waves tossed and churned. Now I was seasick, and my tunes were full of wobbles.

I climbed on to the piano stool the way Keely had.

"Jump!" I shouted.

Mowgli sat and licked his leg.

"Pirates!" I jumped down and made up some scary music for invading pirates. My tunes climbed and leaped, scurrying up into the high notes. *Pdung!*

Mowgli jumped down and nuzzled my bare legs. He didn't understand about being scared.

Dad wanted me to practise the pieces for my piano exams over and over again. He thought that's all I did every time I played. So did my piano teacher. But the music that came out from me every day, which only I heard, was bigger than that.

I remember Mum telling me about shells you hold against your ear so you can hear the sea. But some people don't need to hold the shell to hear the sea because it's inside them, like blood swishing around or the air you breathe. My music is like that.

"Everyone freeze!" I called. I stopped playing and closed the lid.

Now I was hungry.

Chapter 5
Ice Cream and
Diamonds

The Cinderella coach cake sat on the white-marble worktop, a big mound of sponge layers, cream and pink meringue. The back wheels had collapsed and most of the pumpkin carriage had been eaten.

Irena was in the kitchen, gazing at her phone with a plateful of cake in front of her. She dropped her fork and stood up.

I thought of how Eva used to sit chatting on my bed, or how we sometimes watched a funny film together on her laptop. "You want some food?" Irena asked.

I yanked open the freezer. "I always eat ice cream at six o'clock."

"Ice cream!" She sighed like air coming out of a balloon. She slumped back down on the high stool. "Loocas ... I want you to eat good food for tea."

I pulled out the drawers until I found the right tub: Double Chocolate Malt.

If I ate ice cream until I was properly sick, I couldn't go to that drama club maybe for days and days!

The front door banged. "Halloooo," called a high voice.

Vanessa was home. She came tap-tapping into the kitchen in her smart high shoes, pausing in the doorway with her arms full of bags. She wore a blue sundress and a little white jacket. Her flowery scent came into the kitchen too.

"What a day!" she said, all chatty, dumping the bags on the marble worktop and kicking off her shoes. "That train was boiling!" She giggled. "I just can't face that cake."

She looked at me. "Hello, soldier," she said, collecting a drink from the fridge and taking a long gulp. "So, Daddy says you joined a club. Did you have fun? Shall we invite some playmates round for some cake?"

I stared back. Her blue-diamond engagement ring flashed. Dad said it was more expensive than some people's houses.

Her smile faded. "We could get the paddling pool out if you like."

Why did she think I was three years old? I found a lump of chocolate malt. These bits were like biscuit. I scooped it into my mouth. Well, she couldn't make me talk to her, even if she did live here.

She made a little clicking noise in her throat

and turned to Irena. "Has he already eaten some tea?" she asked in a hushed voice.

"He's not hungry, he said. Now he eats ice cream."

Vanessa rubbed her big toe. "I expect he'll eat something else later. So, Irena, how are the English classes?"

Irena murmured something.

Vanessa smiled. "I need a long soak in the bath." She picked up her handbag. "And I'm out from seven o'clock tonight, Irena. We did agree."

Pitter-patter went her feet.

My head felt itchy and I rubbed a place behind my ear.

Vanessa's bags were full of squares of sample fabrics clipped together in similar colours. I fished out a bright red tartan square and held it up. I padded over to Mowgli and laid it across his back. He wriggled until the fabric fell off. My cats never wanted outfits. I'd tried decorating their baskets with Vanessa's samples, but they fell apart.

I went back upstairs and did French practice. I made up a French practice tune on the piano. *Can I buy some eggs? They are in the bath. Do you have a fork? No, I am eating elephants.*

Chapter 6
A Goat Lights
up the Night

I needed to persuade Dad to let me give up that club. But Dad didn't get home for ages.

It was after eight o'clock when I found him working on his upside-down bike at the back of the house.

"Dad, I don't want to be in the drama club," I said. "I have tried it."

"Oh yeah." Dad's voice was tense with the effort of tightening something. *Gnuh*, he went. *Graugh*.

I picked at the edge of my sleeve where a green thread was loose and pulled. A line of bobbly loops appeared. I wrapped the trailing bit round the back of my hand. "I went to the first one today. It was ... very bad." I poked at a loop, trying to wriggle my finger inside it. This jumper was the colour of sick. I would bury it in one of Vanessa's charity bags.

Dad put an Allen key on the ground and looked up. "New pedals. Look at the craftsmanship!" He spun one. "Hold this, will you?" He thrust a can of oil into my hands.

My fingers found the side of the tin, drummed. *Brudulum-brudulum-brudulum-um-um.*

"Lucas!"

My fingers went still. Dad's forehead was creased in ridges. "For God's sake, take that jumper off!"

I wriggled out of the jumper and folded it on the ground.

"Brings you out of your shell, drama," Dad said, stretching.

"It doesn't," I said. "We have to *be* things."

Dad smiled. "When you work at something there's ... a good feeling." I knew what he was going to say next. Dad is a banker; he looks after money and makes it grow. His dad was one too. I waited. "When this family started out in business we were learning as we went along. And now..." Dad pointed to the house.

Should I tell him about my itchy head? I'd always told Eva about things like that. "Dad," I began, "I think—"

"This club," he interrupted, "you're just not used to it yet. Who is your teacher?"

"Avalon Jones."

"Interesting name."

I squinted into the sun. "The hut smells."

"Smells?"

"Yes. It's really bad."

Dad stroked his new pedal. "Lucas, you need to buck up your ideas," he said.

"I might choke. I think the air's poisoned."

"Never going to do you any harm. Find some pals." Dad stood up, rubbing the Allen key on his shirt, frowning. He flexed his fingers. "Look here, my man, Vanessa tells me you still aren't making any effort to talk to her..." His voice was slow now, serious. He grabbed me in a forceful hug, then held me at arm's length. He sighed and his fingers pushed aside my fringe. "Can't see you, my man. Chin up. We need to sort out that hair. You look like a pony."

"Actually, my hair is feeling a bit..."

"You just got a bit hot," he snapped.

"No ... I mean ... itching."

"Record-breaking temperatures," he said, grabbing the bike and whirling it upright again. "This'll have to wait. I'm already late. It'll be dark soon." He leaped on his bike and cycled away.

I checked the cats in their baskets under the window in the kitchen. Tiger was asleep. I stroked Mowgli, put water in his bowl and had a chat with him. He nuzzled my fingers, buffeting them with his head, rubbing his favourite places behind his ears.

Dad had stopped coming up at bedtime since Vanessa moved in. He might put his head round the door when he went to bed, but not often.

Eva always knew I wanted the landing light left on, but now Irena switched it off – or maybe it was Vanessa.

I closed my eyes and lay in the darkness. I scratched my head. I was sure I could smell something, diseases from the hut wafting in the air...

I reached under my bed and pulled out my Glenville the Goat night light from the drawer. He was white with brown horns and whiskers, little squatting feet and cheeks that glowed pink. The red lips had mostly flaked off. He had been Mum's. I found him in a bag of her things three years ago, after she died. Everything else was cleared away. All that was left was this night light, some photos and Mum's red dressing gown. When I was little she used to make up songs about Glenville and say he had special powers for chasing enemies and biting their tails. We used to post my worries inside Glenville's wide mouth so they would all be swallowed and gone. I never played those kinds of games with Dad. I don't think he was there; he must have been at work.

If Dad found my night light, he always put him back on top of the wardrobe again, saying, "Come on, Lucas, buck up." Tonight I gazed at the glowing cheeks and long eyelashes and closed my eyes again.

Chapter 7
Doorbells and
Visitors

Next day, after breakfast, the doorbell chimed. It hardly ever rang. It sounds like a cathedral bell so, even if you are in the shower, you still hear it.

I swung downstairs. It was probably a delivery for Dad: new parts for one of his bikes.

Irena turned, her finger on the intercom button. "Friend," she said. "For you."

For me? I ran into the drawing room as the gates opened at the end of the drive. The girl – the drama club red tights girl, Keely, was marching towards me. I recognised her choppy hair. She carried a little boy. I ran back into the hall. "Why did you let her in?" I shouted.

Irena shook her head. "She is not a friend?"

"Block the entrance!" I shouted. I opened the door a crack and found Keely looking up at one of the pillars by the front door. "You can't come in," I told her. "We are incredibly busy."

"Humph," Keely went. But then she must have shoved the door because it swung wide.

I got such a shock I fell back, and there she was, inside in our hallway, panting.

The boy she was carrying was a toddler, with a round pink face and nearly no hair and a green stripy T-shirt with red shorts. He gripped a massive purple and white lolly in one hand and a bright green dinosaur toy in the other. He grinned. His front tooth was stained purple. That lolly must be blackcurrant.

"I've come to see the ballroom," Keely said.

"Well, you can't."

"Friends!" interrupted Irena. She threw her arms wide, grinning at the little boy. "He is beautiful."

"Go away," I said.

"This is my brother, Robbie. It's only for a minute," Keely said.

"No."

"I need to see if it's true."

"No."

We stood, like drama-club people when the teacher calls *Freeze*. Then Robbie dropped his lolly, *flump*, on Dad's peacock rug, which is a special one that can only be cleaned with chemicals.

Irena gasped.

Keely leaned down with Robbie scrabbling in her arms. She scooped the lolly away from him. "I'm checking it, Rob. You can't have it; it's hairy now."

Robbie breathed in, gulped and then a

scream came out that was even louder than the doorbell. "Eeeeeeeeeeeeeeeeeeeeeee!" It was completely terrible.

I clamped my hands over my ears.

"I will wash it!" said Irena, taking the lolly from Keely. She picked up Robbie. "You come with me." She held the lolly in front of her like a torch and they disappeared down the corridor to the kitchen.

Keely put her hands on her hips. "Well, now you can show me the ballroom. Who was that? Is she ... a babysitter?" She pushed open the drawing-room door. "I'm having a look around. What's in here?" She disappeared inside. "Whoa!"

I followed her. "Well ... in fact ... no ... because ... Irena is the au pair."

In the middle of the drawing room Keely spun round, pointing her toes. "You could have a thousand people in your house. What's an au pair?"

"She lives with us. I think you should..."

Keely fixed me with her marble-eyed stare. "What about your mum?"

"Irena is just..."

"Where is your mum?" Keely asked again.

"You're not supposed to talk about a person who's died," I said.

"Why?"

"I don't know."

"So, she died then? Isn't there anyone else?" she asked.

"Dad is marrying Vanessa," I said. "There's cleaners. And there's the gardener."

Keely giggled. "Does he live in the garden?"

"I don't know where he lives," I said. "He just arrives." I pointed at the door. "You have to go now."

She ignored me. "You can say '*Today I'm going to play in here*'. And you just do it." She ran to the window. "This is a palace. Ginormous. If I lived here, I would wave from every window." She stood there, dipping her hand round and round in a Queen sort of way.

I didn't mean to smile. It's just that she actually looked a bit like the Queen waving – her mouth all tight at the sides, her back so straight.

"There isn't anyone to wave at," I said. "No one can see you from the road and there's walls and the gates. How did you find out where I live?"

"I checked Avalon's register." She grinned.

"Your house is insane."

"Houses can't be insane. Insane is when a person…"

"Come on." She frisked away, out of the drawing room and down the corridor.

I had to make her leave. But how? Her little brother was in the kitchen. What if I ran upstairs to my bedroom? She'd be lost. But then she would be bound to come and find me!

She was like a chimpanzee, leaping along the ground floor, flinging doors open. "Another toilet!" She threw open the door of Dad's study. "That's boring. How long have you lived here?"

"All my life," I said.

"Where's the ballroom?"

I looked up.

"Of course," she said, dashing away. "It's upstairs, isn't it?"

She sprang up the main stairs. "Magic! I love all these carved animals. They're amazing!"

I like the staircase. There are lots of animal heads carved into the wooden banisters, gleaming where hands have rubbed them. I always tap them in a special order on the way up, and then different ones on the way down: the lion, the buffalo, the leopard, the rhino and the elephant. If I tap them and get to the top before I've counted to ten, it's a lucky day. I wouldn't tell *her* that, though.

But she was watching. "What are you doing?"

"Nothing."

"Pah! Don't care." She pointed to the portraits on the way up, staring at the one of the stern lady in the grey dress holding the white dog. "Are these pictures of people in your family? That one?"

"Some are," I said.

"Why do they all look so fed up?"

"That's rude. My dad says in history people … used to … think making a face like that was … nice."

We were at the top.

Keely nodded to the double doors. "Is this it?"

Chapter 8
Sticky!

I threw the doors open and switched on the chandeliers.

Keely had her hands in front of her eyes. She dropped them and gasped. "Oh, wow!"

She darted out into the middle of the gleaming wood floor and began to spin underneath the Avalanche. "Don't say anything," she murmured. "I'm being different." She sang to herself, spinning slowly then quickly.

She stretched her arm out and, for a second, she looked like a queen again. "When I met you I thought you were a girl," she said.

My mouth opened and shut. I touched the hair at the back of my neck. I had been growing it and no one had noticed. We weren't allowed long hair at school.

Keely had stepped up beside the piano.

"Don't," I said.

From the door at the other end of the ballroom Irena appeared with Robbie. He toddled across the floor like a wind-up toy.

Keely patted the piano lid. "Look at this, Rob." She hauled her small brother up next to her on the stool.

A pain started behind my eyes. "You mustn't!"

"Keep your hair on. I'm only looking at it!"

"I mean it. Don't touch it!"

Keely stared back. Slowly, deliberately, she opened the piano lid. One hand reached out and she pressed a note. It rang out everywhere. *Beeeee.*

The note sounded inside me.

Robbie giggled, and, next thing, his hands were all over the piano. *Plong-plong-pling-bum-ping-bong-plong-plong-plang.* His sticky hands!

Inside me I heard chandeliers smash, coming down *crack-crack-crack.* "Get out!" I shouted. "He's ruining it!"

The whole ballroom echoed.

I rushed at them, threw their hands off and slammed down the lid. "Get out! Get out!" The piano echoed.

Robbie started crying.

Keely leaped off the stool. "It's only a piano!" she shouted. She hauled Robbie away.

"No ... no ... it's ... it's ... not!" I flew at them. "You mustn't touch it. You don't understand!"

Keely had Robbie by the hand now. They set off to the door.

Next minute they were gone and Irena stood

with her hands on her hips, shaking her head from side to side like one of those toy dogs in the back of cars.

"You go away too!" I screamed. "You let her in!"

Chapter 9
Butcher Bill

I ignored Irena all the way through lunch. She had told Dad about all the ice cream I'd been eating. Now he had given her a list of my meals and she had to text him if I didn't eat sensibly. Well, I could still raid the ice cream when she wasn't in the kitchen.

Even after the horrible morning, I had to be back in drama club that afternoon, back in the baking-hot hut. Back with *her*!

Unless ... I wondered about pretending to be ill. But then I'd just be stuck with Irena and nothing to do. Vanessa was walking around the house with a decorator, discussing all the things she wanted painted and changed. There was nowhere to be.

✗

The drama club were all in a circle on the floor when I got there. I slid into a space opposite Keely. When I caught her eye she stuck her tongue out.

Avalon said, "We're going to plan a show, invite an audience. The whole shebang!"

This club was getting worse.

We had to imagine being a person in a village. Everyone shouted out ideas.

Keely was wriggling, all excited. "Oh, so there

could be a bakery with its own café. Like Bakewell, that's my mum and dad's café."

I stared hard at her.

They all went on, arguing and laughing. Avalon didn't seem to care. She was such an odd teacher. If she was in my school, she would be sacked.

She raised her hand and, gradually, everyone went quiet. "So ... be the villager and imagine your day. Find a space on the floor. It's early morning and you are just waking up in your house. I'll say a time."

We all lay down. Avalon put on some music. It was good; a busy rhythm of guitars.

I looked up at the criss-crossing beams of the roof. The hut was just a big shed really. Maybe some rats came and did drama after we all went home.

Avalon called out, "Five a.m."

Keely stood and stretched. "Oh no, not five o'clock already. Well, time to knock the dough into shape and put my ovens on. People don't want stale bread." She pretended to get dressed.

"Six o'clock," called Avalon.

More people were moving about now. A boy called Teo was rubbing under his arms, pretending to be in a shower.

I decided to be a butcher.

I stood up and pretended to put a shirt on and button it up. I'd never talked to a butcher. What did they eat for breakfast? Everyone seemed to know how to make real movements, even with no real things there. When I copied, my arms were just sticks and my fingers smacked my mouth.

"Have you got wooden arms, Lucas?" Keely called. "Who are you?"

"I ... I ... I'm a butcher," I said.

"Ha ha!" she called.

"Go away!"

"Don't have to."

Avalon kept tapping people on the shoulder. As she spoke her hands made patterns in the air. "What's your kitchen like?"

"Small. And it's quite chilly this morning," someone said.

I waved my arms around. *Please, please don't ask me.*

"Seven thirty," Avalon called.

The music kept playing. Everyone was walking, starting work.

"Let's watch each person and guess their job,"

Avalon called.

Oh no! If I was a butcher, I'd be cutting up piles of meat, wouldn't I? Eugh! I always blush when I'm nervous. I must look like a beetroot. It would be just like in school when one of the masters asked me a question and everyone got fed up waiting for me to answer. Do something. I would make sausages. I held up one hand wide like a sock as a sausage case and pushed my other thumb into it.

My head was swarming with little nipping itches. The feet smell in the hut was definitely worse today. I gazed at a crack, high on the wall at the far end of the hall like a dark jagged tear. Was that there yesterday?

Avalon Jones floated over. "You look interesting. Keep going. Everyone else, stop and watch. What is Lucas doing?"

Everyone turned to stare at me.

I waved and poked, desperately cutting off sausages.

"Are you in hospital, Lucas?" Keely called.

Leave me alone, I wanted to shout.

"He looks like he's cut his hand off," a girl said. Someone giggled.

"He looks really worried," said someone else.

"No wonder he's worried if he's cut his hand off!" Keely said.

Everyone laughed.

A breath burst out of me. My arms dropped. My voice came out small, like a mouse. "I can't do this."

Avalon grabbed my shoulder. "You're just new to drama, am I right? We're all learning from each other," she said. She smelled of something really strong. Not flowers, like Vanessa. Something else. It made my eyes water. "What were you doing with your hands, Lucas?"

I gulped. "Making sausages."

"Love it! OK, let's all make sausages," Avalon called.

No one copied my chopping. Nobody wanted to make stupid sausages. I felt my face get boiling hot. I scratched my head.

Everyone copied and scratched theirs. No, I wanted to shout. That's not making sausages; that's nits. But then I saw Keely rolling her eyes at another girl and they both burst out laughing, scratching their heads and chopping the air. I wanted to wreck their stupid village. Keely was making everyone laugh at me. She was making it worse!

When I was at home later on, I kept making mistakes in my scales and pieces for the exams, so I just played a butcher-chopping-meat tune, faster and faster.

Then my phone beeped. It was a text from Dad. *Busy day. Keep practising your pieces. Must rush!*

I shut the lid. I messaged Marcus from my school, but he didn't reply. Why was there never anyone to talk to? Even butchers had friends.

Chapter 10
Lying on the Kitchen Floor

It was teatime and all of me was still hot. My head felt like a barbecue.

I lay down in front of the fridge with my arms and legs wide, like the dead body in a murder mystery. This was a good place; the tiles were cool. The kitchen rose up around me: the smooth brown cupboard doors and the shiny amber lights. Irena was on the other side of the kitchen, peeling things. I could hear the *whoosh* of the door. Vanessa. Her red skirt swished past.

Why do people walk around rooms when they can lie on cool tiles, I wondered.

"So, how's drama club going, Lucas?" came Vanessa's voice from high above. She sighed. "Are you all right?"

I closed my eyes. I thought of all the mean sausage-chopping kids, and my itchy head that Eva would have sorted out because Eva was kind.

She clip-clopped away without waiting for an answer. I rubbed and scratched the tender places on the top of my head.

"Do you think he's enjoying himself?" I heard Vanessa ask Irena.

"He does not say."

"But he doesn't mind going? Has he said

anything about it?"

"There's a girl. And a small boy, very small."

"Oh, so he's making friends?"

My eyes came open. Through my fringe, I thought I could see a nit. I made my fingers pincers and … caught it. Yes! I studied the end of my finger. They camouflage themselves. I think nits are clever; they will stay alive on this planet like cockroaches even after everything else on Earth has died out.

I could be a natural history programme. Filming could happen right now.

Eva used to pile up bubbly white custardy stuff on top of my head and comb the nits out. "Loocas, not again!" she would say. "You need a haircut!"

Vanessa moved around the kitchen. She was always nibbling at dried fruit. I watched her shoes with their green bows.

"Lukie…" she said sweetly, bending over me, "why are you lying on the floor, sweetheart? Are you OK?"

A smile crept from one side of my mouth to the other. "You have to come down lower," I murmured.

Vanessa crouched beside me with a swoosh of her swishy skirt. "Have you hurt yourself? Show me. Show me where it hurts."

"It's my head … it's everywhere," I said, all sad and weak.

Her face came down. Her lipstick was bright pink today, like chewy strawberry sweets. And her hair, her long hair … a lock of it hung right down. I mashed it with mine.

My voice sounded like a visiting ghost. "I'm watching them."

She was so close. "Watching who?"

I rubbed the hair against mine. "Nits."

Vanessa's eyes blinked and she gasped. The lock of hair whipped out of my hands as she leaped up and away. "What? Where?"

"All over my head!" I said.

She screamed then. *Clip-clop clip-clop.*

The door slammed.

She'd gone upstairs.

Well, she had asked!

And I did talk to her!

Chapter 11
Otter

Dad came home early. He was furious about the nits. "I'm disgusted!" he shouted, so loud that Mowgli dashed out of my bedroom.

"Look at me, Lucas. What have you got to say for yourself?"

I clutched my pillow. "Vanessa asked. I ... told her."

"Stop mumbling." Dad snatched the pillow away and tossed it across the room.

I hugged the duvet instead.

"You mixed her hair with yours then told her it was full of nits. How could you?"

"I've tried to tell you but ... you were busy."

"This is all I need," Dad said, breathing hard. But he'd stopped shouting. His phone rang. "In a minute!" he said into it, ramming it back in his pocket. He paced the room. "Irena is the one you should have talked to. That's what she's for." He stopped, blocking the window. "I won't have you upsetting Vanessa. She's not used to living here yet. She has been working incredibly hard. She always makes an effort with you."

They were only insects, I thought – it's not like they were poisonous.

Dad was still speaking. "I expect you to

apologise." He paced again, filling up the whole room.

"Vanessa doesn't like me," I murmured.

"What did you say?"

I grabbed armfuls of duvet. "It's you she likes. She's just stuck with me."

Dad took a huge breath. "That's completely wrong," he said. "I … honestly, Lucas…" He walked to the window.

"Mum would have helped me," I said.

Dad's mouth opened wide. "What?"

He went very still. "I … she … I am not having this conversation."

He wouldn't look at me. I really wanted him to look at me. "You never talk about her," I said.

"This is impossible," he muttered. "Sort out the hair…"

He was gone.

I hadn't meant to say the thing about Mum; it just came out. But it was true. And why was it, whenever I said something about Mum, Dad acted all shocked as if that was wrong … or bad?

I thought about the terrible months after Mum died. I remembered coming downstairs and pushing open Dad's study door, finding him hunched over his desk, his shoulders shaking. A noise was coming from him: gulping and a sort of thin wailing, like a bird. I knew he was crying but it was so awful to see because he never did. I went to hug him. But the look on his face when he turned: sort of furious and lost. "Lucas! What are you doing here? Get back to bed!" His face was all pulled and wet. "You should be asleep. Just go!"

He couldn't let us be sad together.

Ten minutes later Dad came back from the chemist with some special nit shampoo, shouting out, "Irena, I need you in here!"

Irena rubbed the stinky liquid into my hair, working it through to the ends, and then I lay on a towel with a wet head.

Even the cats stayed away at bedtime. Dad didn't come to check me. I messaged Marcus. No reply. The night was hot and sticky. I liked having a wet head and no more itches.

Irena got up early to wash the smelly stuff off, saying, "Stand there. I am shampooing now." After the shampoo my hair felt sleek, like an otter.

At 7 a.m. Dad marched in my room again and stood with his arms folded. "I am flat out at work. Next time for these kinds of … things, you talk to Irena. Is that understood? And apologise to Vanessa. And no screens for a week. And the hair's too long."

I liked the feeling of longer hair at the back of my neck. Soon I'd have enough for a mini ponytail. Dad had already marched out again.

I just had to stop going to that drama club.

I wandered down to the kitchen. Dad and Vanessa were inside having breakfast. I could hear them talking.

Dad was all soothing. "Poor little Van Van. I'm so sorry. It's the sort of thing Eva always just dealt with."

"He doesn't like me," Vanessa said.

"You need a holiday, babe. Maybe more time with him."

Mwah … I could hear kissing noises!

"I never get to see you!"

"Oh, you are so sweet!"

I rolled my eyes. Lovey-dovey stuff. Why did they do that? I hovered by the door. I couldn't go in now, not with them kissing.

Dad was talking again. His voice sounded low, serious. "Honestly, I never thought I'd have such an odd child. Lucas is so quiet, so moody. And he does such strange things."

An empty feeling made me cold, even though it was a hot day. Dad really didn't like me. I was all wrong.

That boy Byron from my class who had locked me in his basement and pushed my head under in the swimming pool, he'd said I was odd. That's what they thought at the club when they had laughed about the sausages.

If Dad thought I was odd, how could I be more normal?

Could I practise going round and round on my bike so I could nearly keep up with him and then maybe go to the park and do laps?

No. I didn't like the park. He'd never want to take me there.

He said I was too quiet. Could I be louder?

I ran up the stairs. I scrabbled to untie my laces, dashed into the middle of the ballroom and hurled my trainer at the Avalanche, walloping a hanging bunch of ice stalactites. *Bdangggggggg*.

They swung and tinkled. Fast … fast … then …

slower...

That girl Keely had said my house was insane. Maybe I was insane too.

Chapter 12
Wishing

Next morning Gladstone House was full of the smell of a special tomato breakfast that Irena was frying. She didn't speak to me. My cats were in a wild mood. Tiger hissed at me for trying to stroke him and Mowgli kept running away. That afternoon, at the club, Keely was laughing with some girl called Rosie. I glared at her but I'm not sure if she noticed. I drummed, gazing out of the hut windows at the bins.

I needed to be a loud exciting butcher, quickly. Or run to the toilet and stay there.

Keely put on a wobbly cracked voice. "I've changed characters. Now I'm Mrs Eglantine. I live near the church. I have to walk with this stick because I'm ninety-seven."

"Who haven't we talked to?" Avalon's eyes flitted around. They landed on me. "So, you're still the butcher, Lucas. Am I right?" she asked gently.

I gulped.

"And your name?"

My mind went blank. "Butcher ... um, Bill." I said it again, loudly. "Bill!"

"And have you had a busy day, Bill?"

"Erm, no," I said.

"Why's that?"

I pushed aside my fringe. "Um…"

Round the circle, everyone shuffled in their chairs.

"Maybe he couldn't get in his butcher's shop this morning," Bobbie suggested. "He could have lost his key."

"Maybe the sausages were bad?" Connie said, giggling.

They were still laughing about the sausages.

"Maybe he turned vegetarian," Soren chipped in.

More laughs.

"OK, all of you, up you get," said Avalon. "Each time I say stop, you talk to someone."

I made sure to avoid Keely. She was hobbling round the circle rubbing her back.

"Stop!" Avalon called.

I was beside Connie. She had on lime-green shorts and a stripy green and yellow T-shirt. Her hair was braided into loops and knots. She was the one who had laughed at me.

"Hi, Mr Butcher Bill," she said. "I saw you trying to get inside your shop."

"Oh," I said.

"Did your key break?"

"Yes."

"Did you get in?"

"Yes."

"Can I come and buy some sausages then?"

"Yes."

She hopped from foot to foot. "You're supposed to talk to *me* now," she said.

I gaped at her. "I … I … I can't remember who you are."

"Don't bother!" she said. "I'm finding someone else." And she stalked away.

Then Alan came bounding up. I stepped back to look at his long dark hair; his fringe came right down like curtains. It was thicker than mine.

"I'm a ghost," said Alan. He had a strong way of standing, puffing his chest out. He was in a grey sleeveless hoodie, even though the hut was so hot. "I'm actually dead," he said, rearranging strands of black hair over his eyes.

Were we allowed to be ghosts? Maybe a ghost wouldn't have to do much. Maybe there could be two ghosts.

We stood. Alan was chewing gum. I wished I had some.

"You're funny," he said.

"Oh," I said.

Nobody ever said I was funny at my school. Funny was better than odd, wasn't it?

Back in the circle Avalon asked everyone to think of places in the village.

People called ideas – shops, school, pub, cricket pitch...

Avalon kept nodding, asking for more suggestions, saying, "Wow ... great."

I thought of a football pitch. I didn't say anything, though.

"A well," Keely said.

"Oooh. A well. That could work."

"It could have ivy all round the sides and be hundreds of years old," said Sam.

"Great!

"Could it be a wishing well?" Keely asked.

"Ooh, nice one, Keely. A village with its own wishing well."

Everyone sat forward, even Alan.

"A well that would grant wishes. Something special you really want," Avalon said.

"It's dried up. It's got a secret, though," Alan said. "If you get in, you never get out. It murders people and sucks their blood."

There was a pause.

"Mmm. That's quite extreme, Alan," Avalon said. "Let's each come up with a wish. And you can't wish for more wishes. That's cheating."

"Unlimited ice cream," Rosie said.

There was a murmur of yeahs.

"No, think about it properly," Avalon said. "Bring the wishes to the next drama club."

I walked home beside Irena thinking about the wish. In stories, people wished for money or jewels.

✗

Later I sat at the piano, watching the cats play in and out of the curtains. I couldn't think of any wish at all. Then my fingers made up a thundering tune and my wish turned into a curse. *I wish ... one day in the middle of town that hot smelly drama hut falls down.*

I sang it at the top of my voice, then stopped; something bright green was sticking out from underneath Tiger's paw.

I picked it up. It was Robbie's green plastic dinosaur.

Chapter 13
Bakewell

e o'clock the next morning Irena and I stood
side Keely's parents' café.

I didn't need to go in. I could post the dinosaur
through that blue letterbox in the door. But I
wanted to see where *she* came from.

"Go away for ten minutes," I told Irena.

Irena didn't go. She sighed. "Your father said,
'Stay with Lucas.'"

"No! Leave me alone. Please. Ten minutes."

"Rude boy," Irena murmured, walking away.

I stared through the window. It had big leafy
plants and a pile of children's books on the
windowsill.

Each time the door opened there was a *dring*
and a burst of voices.

I jingled the coins in my pocket. When a lady
in a red dress went in I followed her and stopped
in the doorway.

The café wasn't big, about the same size as our
kitchen. Customers were queuing for bread and
people sat at tables, with buggies and shopping
bags piled up.

But the really important thing was ... the smell!
I breathed. It was the best smell ever. Not just
bread – cakes, butter, biscuits, pies – all stirred

up, filling the air. When I closed my eyes my mouth watered.

"Excuse me," someone said, pushing past me to join the queue.

I slid into a corner and my brain forgot the world; I was just a nose.

Cafés are as busy as stations. Along from my corner, behind the till, a metal sign said **You don't have to be mad to work here, but it helps.** I liked the odd little stained-glass lamps and the laundry racks hanging from the ceiling wrapped round with coloured lights. I counted eight tables, with flowers in jam jars and flowery teacups and saucers that didn't match.

The woman serving behind the counter had a long floury apron and a jolly face – pink and hot. She looked like Keely. She seemed to know a lot of customers by name. "Your usual? Do you want it sliced?"

On the beautiful steaming racks there were so many kinds of bread – sourdough, granary, bagels, rye and all sorts of different toppings on the cakes.

"Oh, go on," said a mum with a baby in her arms.

"I shouldn't," laughed another, licking her fingers and helping herself to a forkful of pink iced cake.

The queue was growing. The last thing people asked for was always the treat – they had been standing breathing in the smell and they had to have something to take home that smelled like that. "I'll have a granary and sunflower loaf, sliced, and six of the small batch rolls … and, ooh, two jam doughnuts."

I noticed a piano in a corner with bags piled on it. It was painted with bright red and yellow flowers, as if it wasn't a piano at all.

A man came out of the kitchen with a steaming tray, slotting it on to the rack beside me. These cakes were spirals, with raisins oozing juice on to the paper. A caramel smell wafted up.

I would buy a cake. I felt around in my pocket for my coins.

But then a lady with white hair and big dangly earrings popped out from near the till and came marching towards me. I was trapped.

"Hi there!" she said. She was talking to me, definitely.

My heart beat fast.

"You've not been in before. Robbie saw you from the kitchen. Are you a friend of Keely's?"

That's when I noticed Robbie, standing by the lady's knee, his hair plastered to his head, pointing frantically at me.

"I ... no ... yes." I felt in my pocket and pulled out the green diplodocus. "Robbie left this."

Chapter 14
Bitspurn

Robbie's face lit up. He snatched the dinosaur.

The woman nodded and smiled. Her white hair was quite tall and frizzy. "Great. So, I'm Keely's gran. Key question, do you like flapjack?"

She had a strong voice and the same stare as Keely.

My throat dried up. "It doesn't matter. I'll just go…"

But Keely's gran was blocking my way. "You haven't told me your name," she said, smiling.

"Um … Lucas."

"Well, Lucas, I've twenty squares of overcooked flapjack in the kitchen and no one to eat them. So, it's an emergency."

"Oh," I said, staring at her big dangly earrings rather than her eyes.

An emergency was a bad thing, so why was she smiling? How could flapjack be an emergency?

"Wait with Robbie," she said, plonking Robbie on a child seat at the nearest table. "Make sure he doesn't wobble off. Are you going to be a big boy and sit with Lucas?"

And then she rushed away, pushing through the swinging doors behind the till.

I looked at Robbie, remembering his sticky

hands. His bottom lip quivered. *Oh no, don't scream!* "She'll be back in a minute," I whispered.

Keely's gran came back with a big metal tray. The flapjack looked like the surface of the moon, except brown. "See which squares are eatable. Just leave a bit for Keely to hoover up. Will you do that for me?"

She used a big flat tool like a paddle, working it round the sides of the tray, lifting up triangles. The other woman, with the red face and curly hair, came over, rubbing her hands on her long apron.

"This is Lucas, a friend of Keely's," Keely's gran told her.

"No, I'm not really..." I began.

She smiled. "I'm Nicky, Keely's mum. Good to meet you."

I tried a bit of flapjack. It tasted of caramelly darkness.

A man with a ginger beard in a white apron popped out through the swinging doors, and the lady from the till put her arm round him. "So, you're a friend from the drama group?" he called. "I'm Jim, Keely's dad." He had floury eyebrows. He dusted Robbie. "Who's my messy boy? Look at the state of you, Robs. You look like you've been dipped in a crumb machine."

Keely's mum and dad went away, asking Gran about something. Robbie's face was all pink. His fingers were in the tin, poking loose bits.

"My bit's burnt," I told him.

Robbie did a big swallow. "Bitspurn," he said.

The shop windows were steamed up. Someone propped open the door with a metal chicken.

Why had they all gone away? What if Robbie fell off the chair or hurt his hand? They shouldn't have put me in charge. I should call Keely's gran and go. Flapjack stuck my teeth together, but in a nice way, making my cheeks fat. Each time I ate a bit, I let the sweetness leak around my mouth.

"Dis," Robbie said. He shunted sticky lumps around the tray. Mowgli was like that, with a busy paw. "Dis," Robbie said again, breathing hard. His top tooth poked over his lip.

"Flapjack," I said slowly.

Keely's gran put some milkshake on the table. Banana. I sipped a bit. It was good. I would finish it and then go.

Robbie was still muttering things. Not proper words. "Brum" and "breem".

"Flap," I said.

"Brum," said Robbie and grinned.

"Jack," I said.

Robbie giggled. "Brum."

"Flap brum, jack brum," I said.

Robbie laughed.

If I hadn't been there, Robbie might have just put the tin on his head.

Keely appeared in the café doorway with two shopping bags. She saw me, scowled and marched up. "Why are *you* here?"

"I brought this," I said, pointing to Robbie's dinosaur, now sitting in the tin.

"You could have given it back to me at drama club."

"I thought he might want it now," I said through a mouthful.

"So, why are you having flapjack then?" she demanded.

"Your gran asked me."

Keely pinned me with a stare. "I'm not your friend."

I felt myself go hot. "I'm not yours either."

She nodded. "What's the flapjack like?"

I swallowed. "It's … it's very good," I said.

Chapter 15
Sweets, Beads
and Froth

All through the weekend I couldn't stop thinking about the café. That amazing, warm cooking smell. Home never smelled like that. Nobody cooked real cakes from real ingredients. Dad hated cooking and Vanessa ate like a rabbit: little handfuls of things she nibbled when she was on the way to somewhere else.

But the worst thing about home was the wedding planning. There were catalogues and shiny pictures of brides in magazines everywhere. Dad and Vanessa talked about weddings all the time: how many people to invite, all the food they would have. Vanessa gazed at her phone and passed pictures to Dad. "Mmm, lovely," he always said, and passed the phone back. No one ever showed me any of it. I just sat there, dreaming about cakes – especially those caramelly oozy spiral ones.

Then Dad said he had a surprise plan for us. "A day out is what we all need!"

"Can I stay here?" I asked. "Please, Dad?"

But Irena had the day off and Dad said, "No discussions," and "Let's take the Ferrari, babe." He rushed us into the car. "This'll get you used to the idea, Lukie," he said, as I did up my seat belt.

"It's a wedding fair!"

Music blared out of the car's speakers and Vanessa and Dad sang along while I sat in the back. A fair. I liked fairs. I liked going on ghost trains and water rides. Would this fair have rides like that? Did people want things like that at weddings?

✗

We parked beside a country house and crossed the car park to go inside a massive white tent.

We followed the crowds through a huge flowery arch and I looked around. Smooth music played. There were people and signs everywhere… **Floral trends. Balloons and table decorations. Let us take the worry out of your special day.**

It was like a big market – nothing to do with fairs. That was just a lie!

Dad said, "Van Van, I need to be home by four. Until then I'm all yours." That was five hours away! And he was on his phone already, going, "I need to take this, babe. I'll follow you." He grabbed my arm. "Stay with Vanessa for me, Lucas."

For the first hour Vanessa kept telling me where to wait. "Sit there. How about those chairs?" she said. Or: "I'm moving to that rainbow stand …

that balloon stand ... that one with the pyramid of glasses..." She kept leaving me and plunging right to the back of the stalls. If I set off to follow her, people looked worriedly at me. They didn't want a kid in there. There wasn't anyone my age, just really excited couples like Dad and Vanessa with laptops and lists and bags full of leaflets.

The sweets were good – foil-wrapped ones in huge sparkly bowls or pastries stacked in pyramids. I edged near a glittering bowl of shining chocolates in purple, blue, orange and red wrappers. A smart woman in a stripy jacket rose up behind them. "You are with someone, aren't you?" she asked, frowning. "Mummy and ... Daddy?"

I shook my head, then nodded.

"Because the sweets are for real clients."

Vanessa was still at the back of the stall on a sofa, pointing at something on someone's laptop.

"I'm ... I'm with her," I said.

"Oh," said the woman doubtfully. "Why didn't you say?"

"Because you said... She's not my..." I tried again. "She's with my dad."

I pointed. Dad had gone to join Vanessa. She

reached up and her arm circled him, and he sank down to sit beside her.

The stripy jacket lady looked pleased now. She held out a yellow sweet, which wasn't the one I wanted. "Bet you're excited. You'll get to be a page boy."

"Excited?" I backed away towards the stall entrance beside lots of pots of yellow flowers. I tripped. The tent spun. My hands grabbed out as I fell and I lay holding a handful of stalks. Shreds of flowers were sprinkled around me. The woman watched me get up. I thought she might want the flowers back, so I handed them to her. She scowled. I walked very carefully further away, feeling her eyes boring into me.

Half an hour later we were only three stalls further down. Crowds of people swept past the whole time. Dad got another call and leaned against a fancy pillar, talking crossly.

Vanessa was studying a tray of food with an assistant. "How many mini pastries can one person eat?" I heard her ask.

I was hungry. There were huge queues for all the food places.

"Dad. Dad, I'm hungry," I said.

"She won't be long. Women, eh!" Dad said, and went back to his phone call.

Nobody cared about me being here. Dad didn't. He didn't even want to look at the things himself either, just wanted to rant into his phone here instead of ranting into it at home. He had really just brought Vanessa. I was an extra.

Maybe I could make a lunch from the samples.

I ate a mini hot dog from a tray, and then another. "That's enough, sonny," the waiter said.

My throat had gone dry. I thought of asking for a drink, but he didn't look friendly.

I ate a meringue with frosted gold pretend fruits. It was lovely.

My throat felt very tickly now. All the drinks were cocktails and I definitely wasn't going to drink those.

I realised I could eat one sample and nobody minded, but I had to eat it carefully and not stuff it down as if I was hungry, which I was. If I ate more than one, the staff would look cross and move away.

Beside me was a silver plate packed with little pancake things with what looked like cream and bits of dark jam on them. I hovered my hand over them, chose a big one, scooped it up and popped it in my mouth.

Argh! Eugh! I gagged. It wasn't jam at all: it was fish! Smoky fish, with beads and froth.

A man in a shiny blue suit was watching from the other side of the stand. I grabbed a leaflet covered in bauble pictures and spat everything into it, then darted away, past rows of stalls, desperate for somewhere to throw the wet leaflet ball. I sped up round a corner and found myself in a huge crowd. "I can't find the cookery demonstration," said a woman in a grey hat, carrying a small white dog. "Is that where you're going?"

"No," I said.

She disappeared into the crowd.

I spotted a container at the end of the aisle with green leafy plants in it and dropped the gooey leaflet ball in. I rubbed my mouth, wishing the taste of the fish jam was gone too. Now I had streaks of black all over my hands from the wet leaflet.

I hadn't noticed the number of the stand we had been in. They all looked the same. I wandered about and checked my phone. The battery was dead.

A lady in an orange T-shirt appeared beside me. "Are you lost? Did you come in on your own?" she asked.

"No!" My mouth was full of horrible tastes.

The lady's fingers closed round my arm. "There's a meeting point for unaccompanied children."

"I'm not unaccompanied."

She wouldn't let go.

"Leave me alone," I said, speeding up.

"What are those dark marks around your mouth?" she asked.

I put my hand to my face. "It must be some leaflet that came off," I said.

"This way." She steered me up an aisle of flowers. I found myself gathered up beside a curved stall where lots of orange T-shirt people swarmed up and said, "Don't worry, we'll put a call out."

I stood beside two little kids who must have been about three years old. Someone handed me some lemonade.

And then Dad arrived at the desk with a cross face. He thanked the orange T-shirt people. "I'm so sorry!"

"Where have you been?" He squinted at me. "Lucas, have you been drawing round your mouth with some pens or something?"

"My phone died… I ate…" I started to say.

He scowled. "Grow up, Lucas!"

Something burst inside me. Why did Dad never listen?

"I completely hate weddings!" I shouted.

Chapter 16
Mowgli

On Monday morning my cats wouldn't play. Mowgli didn't come when I called him and Tiger was snoozing. No wonder; it was too hot to do anything. I wandered around; I lay on the grass and watched the gardener, Mr Sutton, pruning the hedges; I lay on a sofa and watched Irena ironing; and I lay on the carpet and watched a woman measuring the sofas in the drawing room for new covers.

At drama club we had to put wishes in the well for our village characters. I didn't know what Bill the Butcher would wish for except better knives or more meat to chop. What would the gardener wish for at Gladstone House? What would Irena wish for? More evenings off, I decided. And a stronger back for Mr Sutton, because he always said "Gaww, me back's killing me!"

We were all meant to have a turn saying our wish but Avalon forgot me, so I didn't say a butcher one in the end.

I couldn't imagine a real wishing well at Gladstone House. If we had one, I think Dad would just have filled it with soil and made it into a big flowerpot.

✗

That evening was supposed to be Irena's night off. I ate the pasta she had made while she was chatting on her phone and laughing.

Dad should have been home. He sent me a message instead – *Stuck in town.* Sad face. Then Vanessa came home, waving her phone.

"Irena, I've just had a call from a work colleague, and I need to pop out."

"Tonight is my night off," Irena said.

"Usually yes, of course, Irena. But today..."

Vanessa rushed around the kitchen, gathering armfuls of her fabric samples from the backs of the chairs into a pile. She began folding them and putting them in see-through plastic sleeves. "Has he eaten?" she asked, waving towards me.

Irena said. "Last week I did extra days. And Lucas's father had a late meeting on Friday night."

"Oh dear, did he?"

"Au pairs have time off. It is normal," Irena said.

"I can't change my plans, I'm afraid," Vanessa said.

Once Vanessa had gone, Irena sighed. "My cousin had a baby yesterday. I should have been there," she said, and she disappeared upstairs.

Dad called my phone, all fast and organised.

He sighed loudly when I didn't answer quickly. "French ... piano practice ... good man..."

I went to say goodnight to the cats. Tiger climbed out of his basket and nuzzled my hand, then climbed back in again. Mowgli was lying in his basket too. He didn't chirrup the way he normally did, just lay still. He looked odd; his head didn't come up to look for me. I knew straight away that something was wrong. His eyes rolled. He was so floppy; when I picked up his paw, it dropped back limp.

I checked his dish. There was still food in it. Had he had been feeling ill all day? Was that why he wouldn't come out this morning?

Nothing must ever happen to Mowgli.

Dad should be home by now; it was in the diary.

I ran upstairs and tap-tapped on Irena's door.

"Not now, Lucas," called Irena. "I'm tired. I am talking to my mother."

I went downstairs, picked up Mowgli and carried him to Irena's door. His bones felt like twigs and his fur was damp. He seemed to have shrunk.

"Nobody else is here," I pleaded outside the door. "Please come out, Irena."

Close up, Mowgli's eyes had dried flakes of

stuff at the corners. And they were glassy. I laid him gently down again on the carpet beside the bathroom and thumped on Irena's door. *Bang, bang.* "Mowgli's ill," I called. "I don't know what to do."

The door flew open. Irena was in a long T-shirt, like a person going to bed.

I pointed at Mowgli all flopped on the floor. "He's really sick, Irena."

"Oh no!" she said, kneeling down beside him. "I am so sorry." She sighed. "Where is your dad?"

"He's late," I sobbed.

She went inside her room and came out with her phone. "I think … do you know the number for the animal doctor?"

I remembered the vet who did the injections when the cats were kittens. I waited while Irena phoned them, stroking Mowgli, whispering over and over, "You're going to be OK. We're going to help you."

We got the bus.

✗

At the vet's, they told us Mowgli needed a big operation. I wanted to stay with him. I could have slept next to the crate, so he would see me the minute he woke up. He would hate the chemical smell. I could have curled up in the waiting room. But they made me leave.

"Mowgli will sleep for a long time and when he does wake up, someone will be there," the vet said.

"But it won't be me!" I said.

"Call us tomorrow after ten o'clock."

"We will go home now, Lucas," Irena said.

We got the bus home and she disappeared back upstairs. Dad rang and said he was glad they were sorting Mowgli out and he would "try to get back ASAP".

I sat with Tiger, waiting for Dad.

It got very late. I played the piano, so I didn't think about vets and operations. But it didn't work; my soft slow tune rose like a storm, and Mowgli was sitting alone in a tiny boat being tossed and thrown about on a huge wide sea. I had to stop and shut the piano lid.

Irena came downstairs for some water and found me sitting in the kitchen. "Did your dad come home?" she asked.

"No."

I could only think about Mowgli in my arms,

and the feeling of his bones like twigs.

Her eyes were red and blotchy. She must have been worrying about Mowgli too. "I think … it is a good vet. Your cat will be OK," she said.

"He looked so little," I said.

"Lucas … you need to sleep," she said.

I went to bed and took Tiger with me, but he scratched me.

Dad must have come home after I was asleep.

Next morning, I rang the vet's.

Mowgli had had a good night, the vet's nurse said; he was sleeping, because that was how cats got better. "He's doing well. But there's no point visiting."

"Please can you tell him I rang?" I said.

Chapter 17
Little Fists and
Screaming

Next day, Dad called me down to play table tennis. He was waiting for a big phone call and, when it came, he disappeared into his study and only popped out for a moment to tell me he needed to go away for a few days. "Be good. We'll still talk. You can send messages but with the time difference I might not get them till the next day."

I nodded.

Dad hesitated. "Glad about the cat."

"Yes," I said. "The vet thinks it was a kidney... I don't know what the word was..."

"Yep. Great. All sorted, though."

I wanted to do something to help Mowgli – I kept ringing the vet that morning but there was never any news. I washed Mowgli's bowl and put it away.

I decided to go to Bakewell. The warm smell and the people might make it a good day. Even if I sat quietly in a corner. I could buy a cake ... find Keely. Irena walked with me, then went away to meet a friend from her English class.

But when I pushed open the door it wasn't a normal day at all. Over the top of the busy bustle – people calling to each other, the coffee machine making its choking, blasting noise – there was a horrible wailing sound. The whole café was full of fed-up people. A man in a suit was closing his laptop, collecting his papers to leave. Two old ladies at a table, giving water to a fluffy-tailed dog, looked desperate, and so did the dog.

I saw in a flash where the noise was coming from – Robbie by the swinging doors to the kitchen, screaming, like a firework going off in his gran's arms.

She spotted me. "Lucas, thank goodness. Robbie's been up half the night," she shouted over the screaming. "We think it's a tooth coming through."

I stayed where I was. I'd wanted to tell someone about Mowgli and the operation. Not this. Robbie's screaming was terrible. It split my skull.

"Keely's at the launderette." Gran beckoned me over. "See what you can do, Lucas? I've got a stack of breakfast orders to help with and the dishwasher is only washing cold for some reason."

Robbie dropped his blanket and held out his arms. I picked him up. He was sticky and very hot and a big weight, like a sack of potatoes.

I shut off my ears and talked. I didn't know what

I was saying; just rubbish. "So, what shall we do?"

Robbie strained against me, his legs pummelling.

I hummed a tune – *tarum ta-ta* – and people magically cleared a path as I carried Robbie between tables. One of the customers moved a plant.

Tarum ta-ta... Someone shovelled bags off the piano stool. I sat down and sort of rolled Robbie on to my knees, wedging us in, then threw open the lid of the piano. "Up the river we go," I hummed. My hands found the notes. I sang. "*And we all go up the river, up the river and home.*"

Tarum ta-ta. Tarum ta-ta. I ignored his terrible scratchy hot little hands. "*Tarum ta-ta. Robbie is screaming,*" I sang.

Chords shaped themselves under my fingers.

"*Tarum ta-ta, a train on a track.*" My right hand made bright patterns.

Something changed in the air. "Keep going," someone called.

Robbie's fat hot little hand shot out and moved into the space between mine. I breathed a slow breath out. Robbie's other hand shot out. "*Bong!*" A scrunch of notes. I made a tune for unexpected explosions.

Robbie hit more notes. He giggled, then settled for more mashing. He turned and looked up into my face, beaming.

"*The river is wide and the river is long. And all I hear is the river's song,*" I sang, playing a run of little notes to make the sound of the rippling river, then the wild torrents as it met the sea, and the waves crashing on the beach. Robbie put his scrunched little hand over mine, like Mowgli chasing his toy mouse.

I felt a change in the café behind me. Then clapping started. "Brilliant. That was brilliant!" called the man on his laptop, who had sat down again. "Encore!"

All the customers – the old ladies with the dog, the family having breakfast, two men by the door and the whole queue – were grinning and clapping. Keely's mum and dad were standing clapping too.

Keely's gran came rushing over. "Lucas, you're a genius."

"That was marvellous!" called one of the old ladies. "What a performer."

Robbie was still grinning. "Again," he said, in

a completely normal, not screaming voice, still playing an extra note. "Again … again…"

I played a gentle river. Robbie played his note, waited, played it again.

"You've got a job for life there," said one of the old ladies.

The whole café was smiling at each other and at me. And then there was a noise in the queue, and I saw Avalon Jones there, in her long floating dark clothes and a floppy red hat, grinning at me. "That was wonderful … just amazing! I only came in for a coffee. Your playing is … well, it's delightful," she said. "You love it, don't you?"

"Yes…" I mumbled.

She smiled. "You are such a dark horse." Her hands clutched together. "Do you know, you've given me an idea? You can do the music for our show. It'll be perfect!" She turned back to the till. "A double espresso!" she called.

By the time I went home to Gladstone House, the day had changed into something bright and sparkling. I had played in front of all those people and they'd loved it.

✗

When I was on my own at the piano that evening,

I thought about Robbie going quiet on my knee. I kept remembering and smiling, picturing the hot crunched-up little fists, the stubby fingers testing notes.

I began to play. Suddenly I was crying. My hands were like Robbie's, and another hand was resting warm over mine, Mum's.

She taught me tunes, even when I was really little. I felt as if I was snuggled on her lap, surrounded by the warmth of her. The sound moved around inside me as we both played, her big hands helping my small ones. I heard her happy laugh and her singing too, her voice ringing out around the ballroom. She was right there with me. I didn't want the feeling to ever end.

Chapter 18
Music Man

I rang the vet's the next morning. Mowgli was doing well, the nurse said. No need to visit – "He's in good hands."

When I walked to the drama club that afternoon, it was just as hot and smelly as it had been on the other days, but this time Keely met me at the door. "Gran says you're good at the piano," she said. "How good are you?"

I shrugged.

She gave me a hard look. "If you got a mark out of ten, what mark would it be?" she asked.

"I don't know," I said. "I'm supposed to play today."

She grinned. "Well, I'll tell you the mark at the end."

We went inside together.

The warm-up was about all the things you could do with a paperclip. All I could think of was an earring, but Keely suggested a maze for ants and made everyone laugh.

Light streamed through the hut windows in shining strands. I kept shooting little looks at the piano down at the other end. What if it didn't work?

Avalon raised her hand for silence. "I've got an

announcement. Lucas isn't going to be a butcher any more. He's going to create the music for our show," she said.

"Can he do music about sausages?" someone called.

There was a ripple of laughs. "That's enough," Avalon said sharply.

Everyone was quiet then. "Get settled at the piano, Lucas, and I'll explain what you're going to do," she said.

I felt hot and sticky. Connie looked amused and Soren was frowning. They weren't going to like me doing the music.

I walked down to the end of the hut with them all watching and nipped behind the piano.

Keely followed me down and stood beside me with her hand on the piano top. "I'm like your manager," she said.

Avalon smiled. "You'll get used to this, Lucas. It'll be water off a duck's back."

My fingers were shaking.

"Don't worry, they keep the piano in tune for the over-sixties tea dances," Avalon said.

I played a chord. The piano wasn't out of tune; it sounded thin and clear.

"Let's start with the village. Move around in character while Lucas plays, then he'll stop or play very quietly as things happen in the story. OK, Lucas, you begin, and everyone will get started."

My head swam. I stared at some holes in the floor where the lino had worn away and pressed my fingers to the keys. I had played for the customers in the café; of course I could play here. I had an idea: pretend they were all cats, friends of Mowgli's. Not people, cats.

I watched the others walk around while Avalon called out instructions and my fingers began to play. Keely disappeared to join in.

Every time I felt worried, I made another cat in my head and put them on the floor round the piano – tabbies and stripy cats, grey hairy ones – busy cats all meeting and stretching and wandering about. I pictured Bakewell on a busy day. Runs of notes flowed; everyone clambering round buggies and piles of shopping and the queue stretching out of the door.

I couldn't see over the piano top very well – just round the side. People were walking dogs, buying food, saying hello. *Good morning. Good morning. How is your dog? Much better, thank you.*

"OK," Avalon called. "It's very hot. Let's have a break so everyone can grab some water."

I stopped playing. The club people all rushed to get their water bottles. I didn't want to come out. Maybe they hadn't liked the tunes at all. I found my water bottle on top of the piano, popped off the lid and had a long drink.

Alan appeared round the side of the piano. "Can you do ghost music?"

"I … I … I think so," I said.

He stayed beside me, slurping from his bottle.

I made up some ghost music with a creepy left hand full of twiddles and sliding dark.

"Impressive," he said.

More people arrived.

A crowd formed round me. "Can you play famous tunes?" someone asked.

I played a soft song, then I changed it into a marching tune.

"How do you do that?" someone asked.

"I don't know," I said.

"Have you always played the piano like that?" another person asked.

"Yes. Always," I said.

"I wish I could play like you," Connie said. "Honestly, that's just so cool."

Chapter 19
Cat with
Two Tails

After the break, Avalon pulled out huge sheets of paper and everyone talked about the show.

They all got up and made wishes in the magical well while I played along. A wish for a year's supply of chocolate, a wish for an instant umbrella hat on rainy days, a wish for a pet lizard that lights up to make a torch. I thought about my wish for something horrible to happen to the hut. Thinking of it now made me squirm. How could I have wished that? When Avalon asked me what I would choose, I said, I wished my cats could talk to me.

"What could happen in the story to make things go wrong?" she asked.

"Maybe someone tries to take over the well, so the villagers can't make wishes any more," Teo suggested.

"A villain?" Alan said.

"What's our villain like?" Avalon asked.

I thought of Byron in my class. Last summer, when he had locked me in his new basement and switched the lights off, I had begged and begged to be let out, in the silent dark.

Avalon said, "All of you, think about a villain right now. Think of one thing to say."

I remembered the dank petrol-y smell of the cellar ... the moment the lights went out ... Byron's voice. "There's no point shouting. No one can hear you."

I played some music and they all moved around saying their ideas. I found the villain tune – his evil grin, his hands rubbing together, snarling at the audience. The music was thumpy, gloating.

Alan was fiddling with his fringe so all of it was over his eyes.

"Brilliant!" Avalon said. "All of you, brilliant!"

"The well could have a spirit; like a magic being who comes out of the well and the villagers get a big shock," Keely said.

"Let's try it," Avalon said.

I knew Keely would ask to be the spirit. She sat in a chair, answering questions, doing floating movements with her arms and gazing into the distance.

I started playing the piano.

"I come out in the evenings and sit in the park," she said. And: "I haven't got a uniform, just these wings."

Everyone agreed the villain would try to take over the well. But next time the villain tried to make a wish, the spirit wouldn't be there. Then he would think the magic didn't work any more.

"Where has she gone?" Avalon asked.

A thought popped into my head: Dad saying, "You've been working too hard, little Van Van."

"She's tired. She needs a holiday," I said under my breath.

"They send her on holiday," Alan called loudly.

Avalon clapped. "That's it! The village sends the spirit away on a holiday."

We agreed to make the villain angry so he would run off by squirting water pistols at him from inside the well. There were lots of volunteers for that. I clashed some high notes to make the water pistols squirting.

Then, when the spirit came home, we would all celebrate, just the way I would when Mowgli came back.

"Now we have a plot, we'll polish each scene," Avalon said. "Great day's work, guys. See you all tomorrow."

✗

It was home time. I waved to Irena and waited for Keely by the door.

"I thought … I wondered if, maybe … I don't

know, I just thought…"

"Come on then," Keely said, breaking into a run.

I scampered after her.

Irena followed, calling, "Where are we going?"

"To the café," I called. "Let's buy a cake."

Keely showed me the bread ovens and I met her dad's helper, Ivo. They had a fan in the corner of the kitchen, but Keely's dad was still beetroot red from all the baking.

Gran saw me. "What's happened to you? You look like a cat with two tails!"

I smiled.

Then Keely said, "I have to help my mum now." She walked away, then turned round. "Hey, Lucas, it's eleven, by the way."

I stood puzzled. What did she mean, *eleven*?

She grinned. "The mark out of ten. Gotta go. See you tomorrow."

I wandered back across the Green with Irena.

In the evening, when I was on my own at home, I played all my made-up tunes for the show. I played them at different speeds. I couldn't stop smiling. The ballroom filled with my playing. I definitely felt like I had two tails.

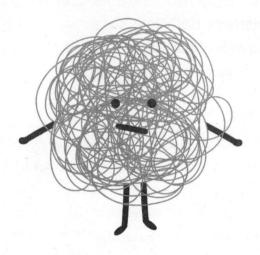

Chapter 20
Rollerblades

The next day, after breakfast, Keely and Robbie appeared. She had rollerblades wrapped over her shoulder. "I need to try these. Gran got them."

Keely thought being in my house was just normal now.

"Irena's busy," I said.

Irena's friend had come to visit. I could hear them chatting in the kitchen.

"It's all right. Robbie can watch. I need space. And the floor here is smooth."

She set off upstairs. I took Robbie's hand and followed her.

Keely turned the lights of the chandeliers on and rushed to sit on one of the gold padded chairs, flinging off her trainers then doing up the long laces of the rollerblades. She glided across the floor, arms carving shapes, looping behind the piano. Her arms wide, as if she might take off, she called, "I am the wind!", lifting one leg, sailing over to the window seat and pushing off again.

Tiger appeared from behind a curtain on the other side of the ballroom. Delight lit up Robbie's face. He toddled off after him, just missing Keely as she crossed the floor.

She was spinning now, floating her arms in and then out. "These are really good rollerblades. They're in brilliant condition. There's only a bit of a scratch there." She pointed to one toe. "No one would notice that."

I watched her. "How do you not feel sick when you spin?" I asked.

"Keep your eyes going back to one place," she called. "I keep concentrating on that gold clock on the fireplace."

Robbie loved chasing Tiger. He crawled after him underneath the piano, and so I followed, shielding his head. He would hurt himself if he stood up suddenly. He never caught Tiger's tail, even though he tried very hard, because whenever he was getting near, Tiger dived away. We came out on to the floor again and Robbie's lip had started wobbling.

"Come and see him," I said. I collected Tiger and we sat down in a window seat. "Look." I put Robbie's fingers on Tiger's back. He wanted handfuls. "Don't grab him – gently!" I showed him how to stroke, hardly touching. "See, that's how he likes it... That's it!" Robbie's face lit up in a huge smile.

We watched Keely skate and stroked Tiger for a long time. Sun poured in, turning the floor gold.

I'd never invited anyone back to my house before. There were after-school clubs. There was homework. Most of my class lived a long way from school. I liked Keely and Robbie being here. Robbie was different when he wasn't screaming … or sticky. I was in charge – like properly in charge of him.

Keely circled to a stop. "Shall we go downstairs and eat something?"

I stood up. "Just … just for a minute, could I try it? Skating."

She shook her head. "You haven't got any rollerblades. Your feet are bigger than mine."

"Of course. I only thought … just maybe…"

Keely did another swinging spin and stopped. She glided over. "Go on then."

"You said the rollerblades were the wrong size."

"You can still try…" She grinned. "These are a bit big on me." She levered herself to the ground with wide arms and sat down. "Phew!"

She lifted her leg, fighting with the laces, and I sat beside her. The boot she passed me felt very heavy. I whooshed the line of wheels, took off my trainer, and pushed my foot down inside. It pinched but I could still squeeze my foot in. I put on the other and stood up. My feet felt so heavy and squashed.

I held on to Keely and tested rolling, one foot forward then back. "Whoa. It's weird." I kept my hand on her shoulder.

"Don't think about your feet," she instructed. "Look up."

I tried to keep my head up, panicked, and looked down again.

"Haven't you ever been on rollerblades or skates?"

"No."

"Just go really slow then."

I pushed off, glided, teetered, tottered, slid and crashed, elbows smashing down. I got up, but my legs went wider ... wider... "Help!" I said. The floor stretched out, shiny and terrible. The windows were miles away.

"I'll drag you," Keely said, sticking out her arm for me to grab on. I bent my knees, pawed the floor and built up speed.

Air whooshed by me. "Hey, I'm doing it!"

"That's it!" Keely ducked away and left me stranded. "Hang on," she said. "I've got an idea."

She dragged a gold chair from along the wall, turned it round then collected another, then a third. "To hold on to." She made a circle of chair backs. I half glided, half hobbled round it, grabbing on, launching myself forward, tottering, then doing it again. I picked up speed and crashed into a chair.

Keely grinned. "Everyone is bad when they start."

I practised a bit more then stopped and took the rollerblades off. "I'm going to get some. I'll order some."

"New ones?" she asked. "Will your dad just … say yes?"

I noticed something in her face. "Probably."

"These came from the Cancer Research charity shop, on my birthday."

"Oh," I said, and then, "they're good ones."

She nodded.

"We should get Robbie some," I said.

She grinned. "They don't do them for toddlers. He's only just walking. He would be so bad at it."

I laughed. "Yes. Yes, he would!"

Chapter 21
Magic Boat,
Magic Plane

"What's on the top floor?" Keely asked.

We went upstairs. "Let's look in here," she said, striding into Vanessa's dressing room.

A new photo sat proudly beside the mirror on the dressing table: Dad grabbing Vanessa's shoulders from behind with a silly face, as if he had just surprised her and she was twisting like a person being tickled. That must have been from one of their weekends away. There was a castle I didn't recognise in the background.

Dad used to tickle me too.

I hadn't been in this room much. Not since Vanessa moved in, just after Easter. We padded across the deep cream carpet.

Keely ran her fingers along the hangers with Vanessa's clothes in their plastic covers. "Smells of flowers, doesn't it?"

She sat at Vanessa's dressing table. "Well, heellooo," she said in a posh voice. "What's in all these bottles?"

"Things she sprays herself with," I said.

Keely squeezed the padded silky purple ball on the end of a sparkly glass bottle. A squirt of spray came out on her knee. She rubbed her arm in it. "Now I smell important."

We shouldn't be in here, even if Vanessa was away and Dad was in Singapore. But otherwise Keely might go home.

By the window Keely found the big sandy-coloured leather chair with padded arms and a footrest. The special chair.

"That's Vanessa's," I said.

Keely picked up the remote handset.

"I love these. They've got one in the salon next door. Let's have a go on it. Come on, Robbie." She hauled Robbie on to her knee. "Plug it in then," she said to me.

I thought about Vanessa lying back in it with pads on her eyes.

"Um, it's supposed to be just one person. It's not a fast thing. You close your eyes." I pushed the plug in the socket.

"We're small. It's only for a minute."

The chair began to vibrate with a hum like electric bees. "Keep still, Robbie!" Keely called. But Robbie wriggled and squirmed, his shorts sliding down and his shirt riding up. Keely pushed more buttons. The chair roared and started juddering. "Oooh!" she shrieked. "This is brilliant."

Robbie's face was a massive grin. Keely

hammered at the keypad, randomly switching between buttons.

"You're supposed to stay on one setting," I said.

"It's a magic boat, isn't it, Rob?" Keely shrieked.

Robbie clambered up Keely's chest and spread himself across the headrest, gripping the top, giggling and giggling.

"Are you the captain?" Keely said. "Do you remember that boat on holiday, Robs?"

The footrest rose up. "Keeelleee!" went Robbie. The chair head flumped back, like the one at the dentist's.

"Whoops!" she called.

Robbie keeled over to one side. I dived, catching him and putting him back on, *flump*. He was laughing so hard his whole body shook.

Robbie kept lurching off and I had to keep piling him back on.

Then there was an odd charred sort of smell, like snuffed-out candles.

"You have to get off now," I said, pressing STOP.

Keely dumped Robbie on the floor.

We stared at the chair. "Vanessa uses it ... if

she's had a stressful day," I said, thinking of Vanessa with her soothing eye mask and her special music.

"My dad would love it. He has a stressful day all the time," Keely said.

I would show them something else, then they'd stay longer.

I took them to the playroom. Keely wouldn't play by the rules in table tennis and when I beat her she said I got the scores wrong. She kept juggling the balls. Robbie found an old wooden plane in the toy box and concentrated for ages on shaking all the people out and trying to push them all back in again.

It was quickly lunchtime. "Come on, Robs," Keely said.

I stood by the front door. "You could come again… I mean, it's a good place to practise rollerblading."

Keely grinned. "See you at drama."

I watched them from the drawing-room window – Keely pulling on Robbie's arm as he waddled up the drive past the fountain. Robbie had liked that plane. Should I give it to him? I waited at the window until the gates closed behind them.

They'd be crossing the Green now.

I couldn't go back in the playroom. It was too empty. I sat at the bottom of the stairs. Irena was still talking to her friend on the phone.

I thought of Robbie stroking Tiger.

And then, in my mind, I pictured another summer day a long time ago. Mum was in a yellow dress carrying a large basket into my room on my birthday.

"Look!" she said. "Gently, Lucas."

She lifted Mowgli out first, and then Tiger shot straight out and disappeared under the curtains.

A big gasp came from my throat. This was the happiest day. In my hands Mowgli was light as a feather. His little face, the dark markings over his nose and his excited eyes.

Dad was there too with his arm round Mum in the sunshine, telling her, "What a brilliant idea." Dad and me were giggling, rounding up the kittens from under my bed and calling them *those little monsters*.

"Do you think Mowgli likes me?" I remember asking.

"Listen..." Mum made me crouch down beside the tiny kitten as we stroked him and all of a sudden I heard it – a sound like a happy little engine.

"Is he happy because of me?"

"Of course," Mum said.

That's how it was.

They would be nearly at the café now.

Lunch would be on the table soon.

Only two hours till drama club.

I would ring the vet and check how Mowgli was. Then I would go upstairs and play the piano. I would find some rollerblades to buy online. I would learn to skate. Then they would come back soon.

Chapter 22
Helping

It was the weekend; Saturday morning with Dad away.

When I rang the vet's, the nurse said Mowgli was eating again. Vanessa and Irena were both looking at their phones. Irena was ready to go out. I was supposed to be with Vanessa today. Dad had found a whole new French vocab booster app and messages kept pinging up.

When I was eating my cereal Vanessa made a little whooping noise. I looked up. "Irena, is there any chance you could be around today?" she asked. "There's a trade fair. They've just invited me. I'll be in meetings and talking to clients. I don't think…" She flicked her eyes towards me.

Irena sighed.

I waited.

"I have worked extra time this week already," Irena said.

"You're very good. We'll give you extra free time on Monday. Look, I'm writing it down now," Vanessa said, leaping up.

"No, it is not possible."

Silence hung in the air. Could I stay at home on my own? No, Dad would never let me.

Vanessa pulled out her purse. "Look, I'll pay

you extra." She counted notes into Irena's hand. Irena didn't say anything, biting her lips, watching hard.

Vanessa grabbed a bag and headed for the door.

"Have a lovely day, Lukie!" rang out from the hall.

I sat looking at Irena. "I'm sorry."

"It is not your fault." She sighed and got out her phone, tapping and muttering.

"Will you still see your friends?" I asked.

She puckered her mouth and shrugged. "I think no…"

"Can I go to the café? I want to."

Irena stopped tapping and stared at me.

"Then you can see your friends. I'll be fine at the café. Please let me. You can come and pick me up later."

"But what will you do?"

"I'll help."

Her eyebrows went up. "You want to *work* in the café?"

"Yes."

Irena walked me to Bakewell. "Are you sure?" she asked.

"You can go," I told her. "Come back later. Five o'clock. Is that OK?"

She nodded, waved goodbye and rushed away.

The café was sweltering hot inside even though the door was propped open wide. Some customers sat outside at tables, some queued down the middle. When I walked in Gran was behind the till. She pushed back her hair and finished counting out change for a customer. "Lucas, I haven't time to chat with you, love. We're flat out. Keely's at the wholesaler's with her dad."

"Can I stay?" I asked. "Please. I want to help."

Gran looked puzzled. I tripped over words, trying to explain. "Irena wants to see her friends. Vanessa has gone out for the day. My dad's still in Singapore."

She smiled, nodded. "Of course you can help, love. I can't promise it will be much fun for you, though."

She tied an apron round me that said "Sweet Treats," with pictures of buns on it. "Could you start by clearing tables? It's endless. You never saw such mountains of washing up in your life."

She taught me how the dishwasher worked,

pulling down the big grey door and showing me how to stack dirty cups and plates. It was so hot inside you didn't need any powder or liquid. And the steam when we opened sort of blew me backwards and then my face went cool because of the fan blowing in the corner of the kitchen. I stood in the blast and my body went chilly and sweaty at the same time.

Gran was right: I couldn't believe how much washing up there was. As I collected cups and plates from table to table some customers asked, "Who are you then, love?"

Gran told everyone, "This is Lucas. He's new."

I cleared tables then wiped them. Then Gran asked me to take people's orders.

When I had been working for about an hour, Keely walked in with her dad and Robbie. Her mouth was set firm. "What are you doing, Lucas?"

Chapter 23
Piranha
Lemonade

"Irena's gone out with her friends," I said. "I asked your gran if I could help today."

"But we can't pay you," Keely said.

I tried to answer. "I don't… I didn't ask…"

"Keely!" Gran snapped, taking Keely by the arm and steering her into the corner. I carried on collecting cups but I could hear snatches, Gran saying, "Don't be so sharp", and Keely saying, "I'm not being sharp."

They came over to find me. "Look, both of you," Gran said. "There's plenty of work and I'm pleased to have an extra pair of hands. And on the subject of paying you … well, we can see what cakes are left at the end of the day. How does that sound?"

Keely shuffled her feet. "Lucas won't know what to do."

Gran nodded. "He's been managing so far, but now you're here I expect you can give him some tips." She gave Keely a hard stare. "Can you?" She went back to do the till.

Keely did a tight little nod and folded her arms. "I'll have to train you. Listen carefully. This is what you need to know."

She sounded like a leader in a battle.

"You have to balance cups and plates but not too many or you'll break them."

I nodded.

"You can do three plates, the most is four. Don't leave knives and forks sticking out in between. Carry teapots separately. Don't scrape everything on to one plate cos it looks yucky."

"OK," I said.

"I haven't finished." She sighed. "Don't eat crumbs because customers notice. Don't touch bread and cakes with your bare hands or break bits off or lick fillings because someone will see. Don't reuse a cake – even if it looks fine you can't give it to another customer. Don't take orders from little kids cos their mums might say no." She seemed to run out of breath. "OK, I'll do the wiping and clearing, you do the dishwasher."

For the next hour we worked separately. Keely would bring in all the plates, cutlery and cups and I would fill the dishwasher. But then she didn't come in the kitchen for a while so I came out and helped Nicky on the till, passing the credit card machine to her, bagging up the cakes and bread, putting little twists in the top of the bags – big white bags for bread, small white bags for buns, and boxes for cakes that might go squidgy.

In the afternoon Gran gave Robbie a little tub of ice cream and then everyone seemed to get the same idea at once and a huge ice-cream queue formed. I gazed over at the piano, but we were much too busy for me to play it.

Keely and me were put on ice-cream duty. My fingers ached from all the scooping. People watched to make sure they had a full scoop so you had to be generous. Choc ices and lollies were much easier.

At the end of the day, once the last customers had left, the door jingled closed and we all flopped down at a table with homemade lemonade.

"Thank goodness they've all gone," Nicky said. She and Jim sat looking through some papers.

Keely's dad let me choose my favourite cakes from the ones that were left.

"I can pay for them," I said.

"No, no, you've been working for us," he said.

Gran rested her head against the wall and took a long drink. She didn't have the scarf on her hair any more and it rose in a wild white frizz. "What do you usually do in the holidays, Lucas?" she asked.

My arms and legs felt heavy. "If we're away, I'm usually in a kids' club."

"That must be fun, isn't it?"

Gran asked lots of questions just like Keely. But I didn't mind. "You learn things... It's just, you don't really know anyone..."

I tried to explain how all the things I had done on holidays with Dad were about being busy, rushing between activities. Those enthusiastic instructors with their big arms giving out T-shirts, rucksacks, armbands and team names.

Gran smiled. "There must be other friendly kids?"

"There's races ... kayaking, archery, diving, things like that. I saw piranhas once, in the Caribbean."

I drank a big gulp of lemonade.

"Lucas, when did your mum die?" Keely asked.

I dropped a bit of cake on the table and scooped it into my hand again. "Three years ago," I said, looking down at it. "I'd just started at my school."

"Keely, love!" said Gran.

"I wasn't going to ask a lot!" she said.

I looked into the pot of yellow flowers on the table. Some were wilting. I reached out and posted them deeper in the water. "It was Mum's heart. It suddenly stopped, and no one knew it hadn't been working properly."

"Did your mum play the piano too?"

"Yes. She taught me. We used to make up tunes together."

"That explains it," Gran murmured.

"Do you look like her?" Keely asked. "You don't look like your dad, so you probably do. Everyone says I look more like my dad and Robbie looks like my mum."

I thought of the photo by my bed, the one of all of us: me held between the two of them in my too-big blazer. "Mum had long dark curly hair… I do ask Dad some things but … he won't ever talk about her. She was quiet…" That wasn't really true; Mum had gone quiet in my head is what I meant. I often tried to remember the sound of her voice.

"No one in our house is quiet, are they, Gran?" Keely said.

"Nope."

Keely sat up. "Did you say you saw piranhas? Wow!" she said. "Could you eat them?"

I thought of a piranha fish with its rows of terrible

teeth, like a mini crocodile. "No!"

"What would happen if you ate a piranha?"

"Don't be daft." I sat up and reached for a drink. "They've got massive teeth. Why would anyone eat one?"

"Well, by accident then."

I was gulping lemonade and now I began to laugh. "By accident!" Lemonade sprayed out of my nose.

Irena appeared at the door. Gran let her in, and she sat at the table with us and had some cake and lemonade. She showed pictures of her family to Gran on her phone. It was odd; I didn't really want to go home, even though I had been in the café since ten o'clock in the morning. "Can I come and help again?" I asked. "I didn't break anything."

Keely's mum and dad looked up and smiled. "Of course," Nicky said.

Gran's voice sounded choked. "You are a mystery man, Lucas. You were a big help. Come any time."

A mystery man. I liked that.

Chapter 24
Whoops!

The long summer heat continued. My clothes stuck to me all the time. The weather forecast was the same every day and the Green was just dry brown sand. Mowgli would be home soon.

One morning Irena signed for a delivery and I carried the box upstairs. I was glad I had chosen the green rollerblades. They looked like shiny bullet-shaped cars. I moved the chairs into a circle, then sat in one to put them on.

At first I mostly just fell a lot. Everything ached, especially my knees where I bashed them, and the heels of my hands where they kept hitting the floor – *smack*. But each time I hobbled to my feet and hauled myself up I kept thinking of Keely being there and saying to her, "Oh yes … rollerblades … yes, I'm good at it now." I would keep going until I could do a spin. Tiger watched, quietly washing himself, leaping out of my way when I skidded and crashed. Soon I could sweep in, curl to a stop and sit at the piano without falling over.

I didn't like the too-big feeling of Gladstone House with just me and Irena in it – the high ceilings, the wide empty floors. Keely and Robbie sometimes called in the morning. I liked that. We might go early to the club and paint the set for the play. Some days I would walk to the café and help out there, collecting stacks of cups and filling the huge dishwasher. I never knew what I would find. Gran would call, "Lucas, thank goodness!"

Irena had a friend called Petra now, who would come to the café too. Sometimes I played the piano. Miss Rollings, an old lady who seemed to be in there all day drinking tea, would pat the chair beside her. "Sit down and talk to me. Don't be shy."

I kept helping her with the sudoku puzzle at the back of the free newspaper. She would say, "This is a fiendish one today."

Keely never wanted to do the sudoku – she would fill in any old numbers just to be finished.

"You've put number three twice in this row," I once told her.

Keely's mouth set firm. "That's the only way it would work."

"But that means it's wrong," I said.

She would throw down the pen. "Then the person who made it got it wrong."

I had never met anyone who didn't care about

getting things wrong like Keely. "It's a mess," she would say. "Whoops! Ha ha!"

✗

One evening, some music was playing in Irena's room and I stopped to listen to it. I realised I had heard the same tune when Irena was ironing in the kitchen too. I hummed it to myself. Later, when I sat at the piano, I copied the notes and made up a left-hand accompaniment. It wasn't hard. It was like a folksong. I went on playing the tune, experimenting with the speed and the chords. I suddenly noticed Irena in the doorway. I don't know how long she had been standing there.

Her face was flushed. Tears were coming down her cheeks. "You play the music from my country," she said. "It is beautiful."

"I like the tune," I said.

"We play and we dance. It makes me feel happy but … lonely."

"Do you miss your country?" I asked.

"Every day," she said. "My sisters, my cousins, my mother. Every day."

Chapter 25
A Hug from
Long Ago

One morning I took out Mum's red dressing gown from my bedroom cupboard. I'd kept it there on top of some of my old books. I found a little perfume bottle in the pocket, and an earring shaped like a parrot.

I hung up the parrot earring on my pinboard. I popped off the perfume top and sniffed … the smell was startling and flowery. *Je Reviens*. French. I looked up the words in Dad's French vocab booster app. It means "I will come back". I put the bottle on my desk beside the photo of Mum taken a few weeks before she died. She and I were eating ice-cream sundaes topped with swirly cream and we had cream blobs on our noses.

I wiped some tears with the back of my hand.

They sent me to school the day after she died. Grandma and Dad had said school is the place for you. But it wasn't. I remember sitting in the sick room and the lady from the office hugging me. I just wanted Mum – to rest my head close by her neck and feel her hair tickling me, that smell that was just … her.

I put on her red dressing gown. I felt very warm in it. It still smelled faintly of Mum but not so much now. I puffed a bit more of the perfume on it and examined the wide sleeves, the belt, the way it came down to the floor. I looked at myself in the mirror. The colour was like blood. I looked too much like someone getting ready for bed, though. But what if it was shorter… ?

Vanessa was busy at her sewing machine. She was always upstairs. She'd had a big order from America for her dog jackets.

I stood in the doorway of her workroom. She hummed, her fingers pulling the fabric as she sewed, the machine whirring with a high *bree* noise, like an insect. She had little trays of bits: scissors, measuring things, printing blocks. Neat hands working together, her foot on the pedal. Sewing must be like playing the piano.

I went inside. "Can I learn that?" I asked.

She turned. "Oh! Lucas, it's you!"

"I want to learn that … I don't know how to do it," I said.

She put her hand to her mouth. "Sewing?"

"Yes."

She held out the blue material she was using, showing me the fancy design in the centre. "This print is called 'Stars and Moons'. I'm making bandanas – like a neck scarf."

"I might make something," I said.

She smiled. "I'd love to teach you." She moved some samples and patted the chair beside her. "I'm not used to boys your age. Have a rummage through here." She held out a bag full of fabric scraps. "You can help yourself to any of these. There are tartans, flecks, spots, stripes, swirls, geometric, sequined…"

I picked out a red and green stripy material. She showed me how to thread the machine. "We'll do a tester; show you what the machine can do. You bring the thread across … down … drop it through there." I fed the thread through and wound it carefully round the plastic post on the top. "That's it. You're a quick learner," she said.

Vanessa showed me simple stitches first, joining two pieces of fabric together. If I pressed down too hard on the pedal, the machine turned into a runaway train. When the threads got tangled, she made a little clicking noise in her throat, shaking her head. I couldn't sew straight. My first attempt was very wonky. I ran my finger along the jagged stitching.

"Everyone's like that," laughed Vanessa. "The

thing is, if you end up unpicking it, it's not the end of the world. Take your time."

I tried again.

It was OK, learning with Vanessa. She let me experiment and if it went wrong, she said, "Whoops. Another one for the samples box. I can reuse everything."

She held up a zebra face on a piece of fabric, sewn with extra zigzag stitching on the stripes. "I make up all my designs myself, so I can tell if they work. This is appliqué. You cut out a shape, lay it on and sew round it."

The zebra was great. She smoothed it with her long fingers. "You and I have got off on the wrong foot, haven't we?" she said softly.

I didn't know what to say.

"I'm not going to try to take your mum's place, Lucas," she said. And then, "I love his stripy face."

"I like the ears and the eyelashes," I said. And then, "Who are you going to be then?"

"I've no idea." She smiled. "I could be like ... a big sister. How does that sound? Just press lightly on the pedal ... not too hard ... that's it."

"OK," I said.

I ran to get Mum's red dressing gown and told

Vanessa about the jacket plan. We measured the sleeves, rolling just over my wrists so I could push them back before I started to play the piano. I explained that I wanted the jacket tails to hang down behind me on the stool. I told her about the pictures of piano players with coats like that on my music books.

"That's a tailcoat," she said.

"Could I sew a cat face on the back of the jacket? And stitch black whiskers?"

"You could," she said. "I love that idea." She laid out the dressing gown, marking the places where I should cut, and pinning where the face would go.

Vanessa was a different person in this room, sewing.

"Why do you make the dog jackets?" I asked her.

"It's fun, I suppose. And I'm good at it. People trust my designs."

"But you haven't got a dog."

She smiled. "No, never did that. I'm too busy to have a dog."

"You've got Dad," I said.

She laughed. "At least I don't have to take him for walks," she said.

Chapter 26
Pins and Paws

I was better at the sewing machine than Keely. She could never remember the threading. She just did some random loops then poked the thread through the needle. "That'll do," she said.

"It won't. You have to thread it properly," I told her, pulling the thread out of the bobbin, which had knitted itself into a nest, and rethreading it for her.

We made bunting to hang above the wishing well by cutting out triangles and sewing them on to a long cord. Vanessa said we could use her samples. Even though it was easy, Keely said, "Can't we glue it?" She went humph and grumped.

"There'd be lumps of glue. It would look horrible. Leave it. I'll do it," I said.

Keely wanted the spirit of the well to have a costume too. She found a red and yellow shirt with stars printed on that Vanessa had put in the charity bag and we set to work altering it. She wanted wide purple wings to go with some green dungarees and she was planning a crown bent out of wire and Christmas decorations. But when we started making the costume, Keely was in a stroppy mood and she cut right through one of the wings. "The spirit doesn't have to be all posh and perfect," she snapped.

The air was tight with arguments.

Keely threw the pins in the air in a shiny silver shower.

I looked down. "Now you'll have to pick those up," I said.

"Ha! I won't!" Keely said.

I put down the scissors. I felt the angry dark boiling inside me. "The cats could be hurt. A pin could go right into a paw."

Keely started scooping pins back into the tin. "Shut up, Bossy Bin Face!" she muttered.

"You shut up, Marble Eye Moo!" I said.

Keely grinned. "It's just so ... boring! I do want the costume, but my fingers won't do neat things. I've never made anything neat."

I thought about this. "Our house is never messy," I said.

Keely looked puzzled. "I share my bedroom with Robbie. Dad just says, 'It's a tip!'"

"If I make a mess, Irena tidies it up. That's what au pairs do," I said.

Keely laughed. "Try living in our house; last week Mum put all the piles of things from our room in three bin bags and exploded at me, 'Right, you've got an hour to put this stuff away or it goes to the charity shop. Get on with it.'"

"What happened?"

"I screamed at her, but she shut the door so she couldn't hear me."

It was strange; Keely's family screamed and exploded, but they all seemed to like each other.

✗

Mowgli had been in hospital for ten whole days before I could bring him home. Vanessa took me in the car to collect him.

The vet said, "Don't squeeze him. He's had an operation and his tummy will be sore for a long time."

"Can I hold him?" I asked.

"Once you're home, but he needs rest," the vet said. "He's still a very poorly cat."

"He hasn't had me! I can look after him now," I said.

She patted my arm. "I'm sure you'll take very good care of him."

In the car, I pushed my fingers through the mesh of his basket. "You're coming home," I whispered.

Mowgli was allowed to sleep in my room. I collected Tiger's basket from the kitchen too because it wasn't fair for Tiger to be alone and Tiger was in my room all the time anyway.

The patch of fur on Mowgli's side had a pink scar as long as my hand. I lightly touched round the edge of the shaved bit, where it joined the proper fur. It felt fuzzy, like Dad's chin sometimes. The rest of Mowgli was so soft.

His head jerked round and he hissed. Mowgli never hissed.

"Sorry," I said.

I hated looking at the bare skin and scar. It can take weeks for the fur to grow back, the vet had said. I wished Mowgli could wear one of Vanessa's dog jackets.

For the first day Mowgli just lay, then he began licking himself, especially the shaved bit. He kept going away and hiding. I wished I could help him get better. I fed Tiger first, then crushed up Mowgli's medicine in his food. I kept topping up his water because he needed to drink more. I wasn't always sure which cat was drinking the water. I put a lot of dishes down so there was water whenever Mowgli felt like drinking.

I don't know if he was pleased to be home. He wouldn't stay in my room, even though I didn't bother him or even try to stroke him very much. Sometimes I wondered if he just wanted to get away from me. Had he forgotten how much I loved him while he was away?

Chapter 27
A Critical Place

When the post arrived I took it upstairs to my room.

There was a card for me, with a picture of a waving cat in a purple and white spotty bow tie on the front.

It said: *On Your Special Day.*

Inside Eva had written:

Have a great birthday, Lucas.
Hope you have a nice day and do something special.
Do you remember our trip to London Zoo last year?
I miss you. Send my love to the cats!
Eva

Dad might remember this year. Eva had bought me a helium balloon of Sylvester the Cat last year and it stayed up for ages. I kept it afterwards, folded in my sock drawer. The cats played with the ribbon.

Maybe Dad would remember.

When I was really small, it was Mum who did special things on my birthday. She decorated my plate with little things she'd bought. My favourite thing was a metronome that helps you keep to the same speed when you're playing the piano. It's a little triangular wooden tower with a metal stick so you can choose the speeds. It goes *tock-tock* in the exact correct time. I thought it was brilliant.

Dad *would* remember this time, wouldn't he? Though I couldn't actually think of anything I wanted him to give me.

We would talk this morning.

He texted a time for me to be sitting at the computer. His face was always frowning in front of pale green hotel curtains. A table with a glass on it was beside him. In Singapore it was evening. Dad's eyes were dark-ringed and he propped up his head with his hand.

I waited for him to say happy birthday.

"How's the cat?" he asked.

"Mowgli."

"How is he?"

"He has to have medicine."

"I'm sure you're doing your best with him..."

Dad seemed to be waiting to say something. Maybe he would say it now... *Happy birthday!*

"Vanessa tells me you have been learning to

sew... She's very pleased. What's brought this on?" Dad's voice had a hard edge to it.

I wriggled in the chair.

"I can't see your face," Dad said.

I looked up.

"Is there a particular reason why you chose sewing? I mean, I'm sure it's a skill..." I didn't like Dad's stare, like someone reaching down from the screen and breathing on me.

I drummed on the chair arm. He'd forgotten. He'd forgotten again. His voice wasn't friendly at all.

"Look at me, Lucas."

I looked up and studied the green curtain behind Dad's head. It was the same green as the vet's table for Mowgli's operation.

Dad sighed. "I just wouldn't want you to be spending too much time sewing, that's the only thing, when you could be ... out kicking a ball..."

Dad was rubbing the sides of his forehead where he got headaches. "Look, I haven't got long. We're at a critical place. Twenty-four hours away from something big."

A critical place ... and something big? It must be a deal. I drummed out the "We Are a Village" tune from the play in my left hand and added something big with the right.

"How's the piano practice?"

"Fine."

Dad was smiling now. This was it. This was when he would say it… "So, anyway, I'm so glad you're spending time with Vanessa. That's great. I know it's been a bit of a miserable summer and you've seen very little of me so far but … well, fingers crossed… I won't say any more just yet."

Then suddenly Dad's voice changed. "Good grief! Turn round."

"What?" I said.

"Pardon!"

"Pardon."

I turned round.

Dad's voice started ranting. "You need a haircut, my man. I told you days ago."

"Why? I like it!" I said loudly. Why did he only care about my hair?

Dad's astonished face plunged towards me. I reared back. "I'm not discussing this. Get it cut or I'll have to text Irena."

There was a noise behind Dad and he turned, murmuring, "I'm on my way."

I stared at the back of Dad's head. His hair was very short and organised.

"Dad, it's my…" I began.

"Right," Dad said. "Goodbye."

The screen went black.

I liked my long hair.

I didn't want to go to have a stupid haircut ON MY BIRTHDAY. No thank you!

When Keely appeared I had a plan. "We're going to cut my hair," I told her. "Dad says I have to."

Chapter 28
Shaving
Operation

Keely grinned. "Can I be the hairdresser?"

"Yes."

We set up in Dad's bathroom. His electric razor was in a padded black case. He'd taken his special travelling one with him. I unzipped it and ran my fingers along a ridge of grey spikes. I pressed the first button. On. Green lights flashed. Vibrations went right up my arm. "Whoa!"

I switched it off and passed it to Keely.

"Did you ask to borrow this?" she asked.

"No."

"We'd better be quick then."

I remembered people describing what they wanted at the barber's. "Leave the middle bit." I opened a wide finger span. "I want the shaggy bit to go all the way from the front –" I held my hand wide over my forehead – "and over the top –" I made an arc – "and down the back. And leave the long bit behind."

"Yes, sir." Keely giggled. "Gran would call that punk."

"It's a mane."

"And the sides?"

I laughed. "I don't want them. Shave them off."

Keely nodded. "I'm going in!"

The buzzing came right by my ear. The hair came off in lumps. It took a few goes because it was so clumpy. My scalp turned cool.

"This is great," Keely said. She smoothed one side with her hand and switched to the other. "Can we do me after?"

My head looked like an egg with a long furry road down the middle.

Irena appeared by the door. "Drinks?" she said. Then she saw us and noticed the chopped hair around our bare feet. "Oh, Lucas!" she moaned. "Lucas! Your dad will send me away."

"Don't worry, Irena," Keely said. "He told Lucas to do it."

Irena laughed, but in a wild, sad way. "Not like this. You must tell your dad it is not my idea." She locked the razor in the bathroom cupboard and pocketed the key.

✗

When we went down to Bakewell afterwards, Gran was serving customers, but when she saw us she stopped and her mouth fell open. "What have you done? Lucas, love, that's quite dramatic." People in the café turned to stare. A bubble of worry started in my chest, like when

I had a piano exam.

"Some of it is completely gone," I said.

"We can see that!" Gran's face was still wild, gasping. Then I wondered if she was trying not to laugh. She was biting her mouth in a way that was making my bubble of worry fill up until I could almost not breathe.

"My dad said I had to get it cut," I said.

"Did he? Never mind, love, it'll grow back." Gran finished serving, rummaged under the till and pulled out a red baseball cap. "Wear this. Just until everything ... settles down. When is your dad back?"

"Um ... I think in three days."

All the energy had gone out of me now. Mowgli must have felt like this when they shaved him.

Gran nodded. "That's quite soon."

"We're doing mine next," Keely announced.

"Oh no you're not," said Gran.

We drank some lemonade. Keely noticed the card in my bag and I told her it was my birthday.

"It's your birthday and you didn't tell anyone?" She seemed completely amazed. She announced it to Gran. "It's Lucas's birthday today and nobody knew."

Gran called, "Are you doing something special today then, love?"

I didn't know what to say. I felt as if I had done something wrong. But how do you make your own birthday special? You can't really. People have to help you.

Gran's mouth wobbled. "This won't do," she said. She rushed away into the kitchen and came back with an iced bun with a candle in. "It's Lucas's birthday!" she called to everyone. "Blow this out and make a wish, love!"

Then all the customers sang "Happy Birthday" because Gran and Keely were singing it really loud, so they had to join in.

✗

When we arrived at the drama club that afternoon, Avalon called, "Hi, Lucas," just like normal.

You couldn't see much of the shaved sides with the cap on, except the bald bits behind my ears. I liked flipping the long bit of hair out under the band of the cap to make a pony tail.

Alan said, "That is a cool haircut."

Connie said, "Did you get a fright and all your hair fell off?"

"Keely did it," I said.

"Oh!"

Keely made the club sing "Happy Birthday". I wore my new cap all afternoon, even though it felt prickly round the sides.

In the evening Keely came round with a bottle of stuff her dad used on his beard. It was brown and smelled of oranges and medicine. "I thought it might make the hair grow back faster," she said and rubbed some on. I put the baseball cap on again.

"Let's check it again later," she said.

"It itches me, with the cap on," I said.

"Well, leave the cap off then. I don't know!" she said. "I was only trying to help!"

The haircut had been fun when we did it. Not any more; my head was stained chestnut brown. I tried to wash it off with lots of soap, but it left a big dark splodge. I looked odd. That's what Dad would think.

I put the red baseball cap on in the evening while I played the piano. It was a present, I realised. I had a birthday present after all.

Chapter 29
Messing About

The next day, I struggled with my tailcoat. The tails at the back didn't lie properly and one tail looked wider than the other. I worked on the cat face for the back instead. The whiskers looked fantastic.

I laid the jacket on my bed.

Before I left home I called Mowgli. He must be asleep somewhere. I checked that his bowl was empty. He definitely had his tablet last night and again this morning. His water was gone. Tiger couldn't have drunk all of it on his own.

We did a whole run-through of the show with me playing. Sammy was going to be the villain. We practised all the parts where he shouts at the audience or threatens the village. I looked around at all the people in the hut. Connie was lounging on the floor. Soren was looking through the decorations people had made.

"It's going well," Avalon said. "Are all your costumes ready?"

Keely was giggling with Connie about something. Then she suddenly said, "Lucas, are you wearing that old red dressing gown?" Everyone stopped to listen. "Hey, are you going to put on your pyjamas with it?"

I sat there, my fingers clenching and unclenching

as they all started laughing.

"Hey, you could wear a string of sausages!" someone called.

It was just like when the club first started, weeks ago: all of them sprawling and giggling at me. I was odd. My head boiled. My face was beetroot red.

Next thing I was out of the hut and running away from them and all their gaping faces. Why did I ever trust Keely?

I ran all the way home and stood inside the doorway, panting. I would find a whole tub of ice cream. I would eat it with the biggest spoon. I would scoop and scoop until it was all gone. I headed for the kitchen.

But then I remembered I hadn't seen Mowgli today. I would check on him first. "Mowgli!" I called in the hallway. "Mow ... Mow ... Mowgli!"

I heard a noise and Keely burst in through the open front door. "I came to find you!" she said. "You left the gate open."

"Go away."

I pushed open the drawing-room door and nipped behind the sofa and chairs. If Mowgli was snoozing, these were the best chairs, because the sun made them warm all day. "I'm not talking to you," I told Keely. I pushed the curtains to the side.

"What are you doing?" she asked.

"I have to find Mowgli." My voice had a sob in it. "Mow … Mowgli!" I called. "He's sick. I don't know where he's gone. And I don't like you any more."

"I was only messing about… Can I help?"

"No!" I checked behind a lamp. "You made everyone laugh at me." I marched out and began working my way along the ground-floor rooms, pushing open doors, my eyes darting into corners, all his favourite places.

"I'm good at finding things," Keely said, following me.

I wouldn't talk to her. Then she'd go.

I leaped up the stairs. I threw open the doors and ran out across the ballroom.

He wasn't behind the curtains.

Tiger came to find me. He weaved round my legs. He jumped on all the beds, chirruped and dashed ahead. I even opened cupboards a cat couldn't have got in, unless someone had helped him.

"Mowgli!" I called. "Where are you?"

Chapter 30
Goodbye

When I reached the third floor I realised that Keely wasn't with me any more. Maybe she had gone home. I checked in Dad and Vanessa's rooms. I didn't think Mowgli would have gone in there, but Mowgli wasn't himself, was he? I checked the airing cupboard and the ironing hanging in the dressing room.

Then Keely was shouting from downstairs. "Lucas. Quickly!" Her voice had a tremble in it. I sprinted down. "Where?"

I saw a dark mass of something behind the coats in the hall.

We shunted the heavy coat stand out of the way.

I fell to my knees.

He was curled up, lying on his side.

"Mowgli," I whispered. He made a tiny "meep" sound and his eyes fixed on me. His head didn't come up to say hello, though. That's why he hadn't answered; he couldn't.

He was floppy. His tummy was rising and falling in little ripples. When I ran my fingers across his back the fur was straggly and matted and his head jerked a tiny bit.

I stroked him, then bent down beside him but

there was no little engine purr. I held one paw, then another. Cold. "Why is he cold?" I asked.

Keely held out a blue fleece of Dad's and I laid it over him.

Tears ran down my face.

"I'm going to get Gran," I heard Keely say. "I'll come back."

Maybe Mowgli needed a drink. I didn't want to leave him, but the vet said he had to drink. Maybe he needed to drink right now. I went to the kitchen and got his saucer of water. I knelt down and held it beside his face, but his head still didn't come up. I dipped my fingers and tried dripping a bit near his mouth. "Do you want a drink?"

He didn't want anything.

I sat in the empty hall. Tiger came and rubbed himself against my back. I stroked him from head to tail, and his fur was all electric and warm but then he danced away up the stairs.

Then I heard Gran's voice beside me. "Hello, Lucas. Oh dear, poor Mowgli." She stroked him under the fleece and looked in his eyes. "Do you think he might like to be in the sunshine, Lucas?" she said.

I couldn't think properly. "Do you think that could help?"

She nodded. "Would you like to bring him outside?"

Tears dripped off my nose.

Gran picked him up, cupping his head. I held out my arms to take him, wrapped up in the fleece with his eyes gazing up at me. I took him gently down the steps and behind the house where there's flower beds and trees. Keely and Gran were somewhere near. I sat down under a tree. The sunlight made patterns on the ground.

I sang to him. "*And we all go up the river, up the river we go. And we all go up the river, up the river and home.*"

I hugged him to me. His eyes looked into mine and closed.

The sun went behind a cloud.

I cried and held him. He wasn't moving any more. He was still. Very, very still.

Gran sat down beside me. "He's died, Lucas, love."

I just sat holding him. His face was still Mowgli: those dark markings over his nose. "Why did you hide from me?" I asked him. "Why didn't you want to see me?"

Gran's arm came round me. "Animals go away to be on their own, love. That's what they do. It's no one's fault."

"I tried to look after him," I said.

Gran hugged me tight. "Lucas, you were the very best owner he could have had."

I laid him under the tree, curled up, all small in the fleece. His body was going cold.

Gran's arms felt so strong and warm. She smelled of bread. A long time passed, and I just cried. Someone gave me a drink of water.

"I want my mum," I said. Time stretched out or stopped. "I never said goodbye to Mum."

"Tell me more about her," Gran said.

So I did.

Chapter 31
The Big News

Dad coming home got nearer. I spoke to him on the phone about Mowgli. He said he'd told the gardener to bury him under the tree. He said he would be home really soon. "We'll sort all this out."

But he couldn't sort it out, could he?

I sat at the piano for the next rehearsal and we practised the scene where the spirit comes out of the well. Keely was in her outfit that I had made. I sat watching the drama club whirl around me, playing for Keely, a dance of being free.

As I played, I was in the garden with Mowgli. Green trees leaned softly over us. He should never have been an indoor cat. He should have run around on grass.

Dad would be on a plane already.

The villain was coming back. My left hand found a slow, dark drone. The drone pounded as Sammy swept in, hissing and twirling. The garden wasn't there any more. There was just a sad dark place.

"Hey, Lucas!"

Someone was shouting. Connie, Teo and Keely appeared out of the mist and their voices brought bright light. I stopped.

"At last! We couldn't get you to stop playing!" Teo called.

I blinked.

"We don't need so much villain music ... just a bit!"

✗

That afternoon, I knew as soon as the door opened that Dad was back because of the cases in the hall. He appeared on the staircase and came sprinting down. "Lucas, my man! I'm sorry things have been... It's been a really... It's all going to get much better."

My mouth opened to say "How can anything get better when Mowgli's dead?"

But Dad was thrusting a new computer game into my hands. "I thought ... a bit of a treat!"

"It was my birthday," I said.

His mouth became set. "Well, there you are then."

He came down beside me. "Hang on, what have you done to yourself?" His lip curled. "What on earth's happened to your hair?"

"I got it cut," I said.

"Good grief. You can't have it like that! Take off

that ridiculous cap."

I pulled off my red baseball cap.

Dad's eyes went wide. His mouth opened in a gasp. "What's that stain on your head? Is that ... shoe polish?"

"Beard oil," I said.

Vanessa came down the stairs beside him. "We can make a hair appointment." She put her hand on his arm. "Richie, it'll be fine."

Dad frowned. His features rearranged themselves. He nodded. "I'm back now," he said. "And, get ready. Have I got a surprise for both of you!" Dad did a pretend drum roll. "I said we all needed a break. It's booked. The three of us are going on an all-inclusive holiday to a tropical paradise in Tenerife. There's an amazing range of activities for you, Lucas. No time to lose."

Vanessa grinned. "That's great, babe. And is it that hotel we picked?"

"Yep. They had space. Beautiful rooms... Spa! You're gonna love it. We all are."

I gulped. "When?"

"Three days' time!"

Chapter 32
Siege

Here was Dad leaping, spinning Vanessa round, her floaty blue and white skirt like a dandelion clock in the wind. "I've booked a week, babe. And we've cleared the diaries ... and Lukie, there's a kids' club. You'll be in heaven; some kind of scuba diving, snorkelling thing. You can start at eight in the morning, if you want. They take you out on boats or canoes or..."

I would miss the show at the drama club. I would sit by some stupid pool with Dad and Vanessa giggling and no one to talk to, or I would end up at a kids' club with a bunch of children whose names I couldn't remember.

There was a terrible breathing-in pause. I couldn't go; the drama club needed me. I was the musical director.

"No!" My shout filled the hallway. "I can't!"

Vanessa dropped Dad's hands. "Lukie..." she said softly.

Dad's face darkened. "I beg your pardon. What did you say?"

I shook. "I can't come. Please can we..."

Dad's voice was a volcano. "*You* definitely *are* coming!"

"I'm not. I can't," I said. Hot tears came out and

I blinked them back in. "I have to be here."

Dad shook his head.

"You can't make me," I shouted. "I won't. I don't want a stupid kids' club!"

"This is not open for discussion. You will be on that plane and that's the end of it."

"No!" I shouted.

Dad's face was red, his shoulders braced.

I bolted away, taking the stairs two at a time, hearing Dad's big feet coming behind me. "I'm not coming!" I shouted, sprinting across the landing and slamming into my room, quickly turning the key.

Block it too. I dragged the chair up against the door.

"Open this door!" bellowed Dad from outside. *Thump, thump.* "Come out this minute!"

My ears buzzed and my heart leaped with each terrible bang.

"I'm not coming out!" I shouted. "I'm never coming out." I climbed on my bed and stood staring at the door.

"No screens … no pocket money," went the voice. "No phone … grounded … spoilt…"

I found myself humming. *"We are a village.*

Tarum ta-ta ... bang, bang, bang... Get stuffed...
Not coming... Get stuffed..."

Finally the thumping stopped. I guessed Dad had gone.

✗

After half an hour all the hot feelings had drifted away. I jumped down. I wished Tiger was in here. And then another thought; no one would feed him. He would be all alone. Would Irena think of it, if he mewed at her ... if she was in the kitchen?

Dad had said we were leaving in three days ... was I going to stay in my bedroom for three days? People died without water in hot places. I drank the water from the glass beside my bed.

Another hour went past. I lay on the bed staring at a wooden glider hanging from the ceiling as it turned and turned.

I'm not going on holiday.

Dad couldn't make me ... could he? I imagined running away at an airport and hiding behind a pillar, dodging round a family with big suitcases and running down the escalators ... *Follow that kid. It's no use – he's escaped.* I would steal one of those loading trucks, zoom across the airport on it and cut through the fence with clippers.

It turned dark outside.

I'm not going on holiday.

I drifted into sleep. Dad's voice woke me from outside the room. "Have you calmed down … can we talk sensibly?"

I padded to the door, perching on the chair. Dad must be very near. "I can't be away. It's the drama club. I can't miss it," I said.

Dad might listen. He might.

"You told me you hated the drama club," Dad said.

"I did but now it's … different," I said. "It's good now."

"You're making this up." Dad's voice rose. "This is nonsense. You are being deliberately difficult."

"No. They can't manage without me. I … I have to be here."

"Like a whining girl!"

"Why don't you believe me?" My voice rose too. "Why don't you ever ask me?"

"This is ridiculous," he snapped. "We'll sort this out in the morning."

I flopped down again on my bed. "Dad!" I called.

It was useless.

Chapter 33
Morning Baking

When I woke again I was very thirsty. My bedside clock said quarter to five. I tipped the glass by my bed but there wasn't even a drop of water left. I found a mint in the bottom of my pocket and sucked it.

I put my trainers on and listened right by the door. Dad sometimes worked through the night. I shunted the chair out of the way.

First the key in the lock … turning it so, so slowly … the door softly opening. I was out.

Was the burglar alarm on? I waved at the sensor high up on the wall. It flashed red, but nothing happened. Phew, Dad hadn't set it.

I had to do something. I thought of the Avalanche chandelier. Imagine the massive bang of the Avalanche falling and all those white crystals spearing deep into the ballroom floor. I could do that. I'd watched while the men cleaned the chandelier, so I knew where it was hooked under the floorboards in the room above the ballroom.

But I would still end up in Tenerife. And Tiger might get splinters in his paws.

I went downstairs.

All the lights were off except a dim glow in the kitchen… Every sound seemed huge. I went to the toilet in the downstairs loo and drank from the cold tap. I crept out and back to the kitchen. The cat bowl had food in and Tiger was asleep.

My eye caught the gleam of the kitchen cooker. I thought again of the smell of Bakewell in the early morning. Keely had pretended to be in Bakewell at the drama club. 5 a.m. she had said. *Put my ovens on. People don't want stale bread…*

Something was going to happen, and the making-it-happen person was me. I realised how to not go on Dad's holiday; everything joined together in my head with the answer.

I turned the knob and gently pushed open the door of Dad's study. I opened the fold-down bit of the bureau with a tiny creak and held it there with one hand while I felt around and collected what I needed.

A few seconds later I stepped out into the early pink sky day and sprinted up the drive. If someone was looking out, they would see but when I checked, all the blinds on the upstairs windows were closed.

The gates opened and clunked shut. I was free.

I crossed the Green. The air felt cool. There was

a bin lorry making its way round and I could hear the crunch as it swallowed the bags lobbed in by the bin men.

I ran all the way.

I went down the alleyway to the back of Bakewell and eased open the door. Keely's dad, Jim, was singing at the end of the corridor. I could hear the clattering of metal things. I slipped inside and hid behind a fridge. I spotted Jim in his long white apron carrying a sack into the storeroom, and nipped through to the kitchen.

Inside were the grey shiny tables, loaded with doughy mounds and twists ready for the oven. The oven was on, glowing orange inside. I remembered Keely showing me how quickly the loaves cooked. I unhooked the heavy gloves hanging beside it, put them on and opened the grey hatch. Heat blasted my face. With a flick of my wrist I threw my passport deep inside. It curled and lit, fizzing up blue then white. I shut the hatch and whipped off the gloves, hearing Jim coming back…

I slipped, panting, through the swinging doors into the café.

Chapter 34
Early Breakfast

I couldn't stop shaking. I sat down on the piano stool in the dim light. I thought of Robbie and Keely, asleep upstairs. The clock behind the till said twenty past five.

My legs felt like jelly. My head pounded. I didn't want to go home.

Jim appeared in the doorway. "Lucas!" He dusted his hands on his apron. "I thought I heard a noise. What on earth are you doing?"

I thought about my passport blazing. Would it spoil the bread? No. Everything gets burned in there, Keely said. My whole body ached. Keely's dad was beside me, his hand pressed firmly on my shoulder. "What's goin' on?"

"I … I … I…" I tried to think of an answer. "I wanted to meet Keely for breakfast," I said, at last. But I was still shaking, and the tears started to drip.

"You're much too early, son." Jim sounded friendly but puzzled.

I cried more. "I am a bit early, yes."

His voice was kind. "Well, you could come back about eight… I could get Keely to text you when she's up."

"I haven't got my phone any more." Thinking

of my phone taken away last night made me remember all the problems waiting for me at home. "I'll just go. I'll come back later." I slid off the stool and looked up into his warm face, the flecks of flour in his beard.

The shop door tinkled. Ivo breezed in and stopped in the middle of the café, staring at us. "Blimey, this is a bit early for opening up."

Keely's dad laughed. "Tell you what, Lucas, Ivo is here now. I'll walk you back. I'll just be ten minutes, Ivo."

Ivo disappeared into the kitchen calling, "No problem-o."

Keely's dad smiled. "You must be hungry." He went over to the counter where there were cakes and buns sealed in bags. "These are yesterday's. We drop them to half price. Why don't I choose you a couple of nice ones?"

We walked back across the crisp dead grass. Early commuters strode purposefully towards the station. Birds were singing. Two cars were driving round the Green.

When we reached Gladstone House we walked together up the drive, but someone was waving from the drawing-room window. Irena. She met us at the door.

"You'll be all right now," Jim said. "See you later, lad. Take care now." He patted me on the shoulder and turned back the way he had come.

Irena saw my bag of cakes. "Quick," she said. "I will bring milk. Go upstairs. Your dad is still sleeping."

✗

Some time later I woke up. My head swam. I saw the empty bag of cakes beside me and the empty glass of milk. I sat up and found my door was wide open.

There were hushed voices, Vanessa's and Irena's, coming from somewhere upstairs.

I didn't want to talk to them. I went to sit on the wide staircase and Tiger came and nuzzled me. He looked for me more often since Mowgli died. I stared blankly at the carved animals on the banisters. I liked sitting here. Staircases are between places.

I couldn't remember eating the cakes. I must have, though, then I must have fallen asleep. I stroked Tiger's ears. "You're missing Mowgli, aren't you?" I whispered.

I didn't hear Dad come down, and jumped

when he spoke. "You're up. Good. We'll need to sort out that hair. And there won't be a lot of packing. It's pretty warm there."

He waited but I said nothing.

"Have you not enjoyed our other holidays together? I mean, you've seen some amazing places... And the sports and clubs? You should be a very happy boy. Why do you never look at me when I'm talking to you?... I know you've been sad about the cat..."

"Mowgli."

"About Mowgli. I don't think you and I always understand each other very well ... all this tinkering about with sewing and then the hair..."

I felt very tired, as if I'd climbed a huge mountain and run down the other side. "You don't know me," I said.

Dad's mouth dropped open.

I couldn't look at him.

"The holiday's for you. Not me. And I'm not coming," I said.

"Now we're not starting this again!" Dad's voice was full of warning.

"Richie!" Vanessa called.

"Just get some breakfast," Dad told me, turning

away. Then he ran downstairs.

I waited. I was glad Tiger was with me. My heart thumped, imagining Dad in his study.

A few minutes later he appeared at the bottom of the stairs. He looked up at me. "Lucas, have you hidden your passport?" he asked crossly.

"Not hidden." My voice was quiet.

He stood looking up at me. I bent my head. "I wanted to tell you…"

Still he stood there.

Words came out of me. "I burned my passport. It's gone."

Chapter 35
Jump at the
Chance

Dad was a cold no one. He didn't want to see me. The rest of the day wore on and I went to drama club and came home.

At bedtime Dad appeared in my doorway. "I've been talking this over with Vanessa and Irena." He rubbed the side of his head. "When I booked us a holiday I thought you would jump at the chance."

Jump at the chance.

"Are you listening to me, Lucas?"

"Yes."

Dad looked very tired. Like a balloon with no air. His forehead had lines upon lines. I pictured my passport in the oven. There would be nothing left of it now. Maybe it was inside some bread, like fine sand. Someone would think it was wholemeal and eat it.

Dad was all sad and flat.

"Vanessa and I have decided to go on the holiday on our own. Irena will look after you. I can't imagine why you want this, but you clearly do." He was all closed up. "I've already taken time off… It can't be helped."

He hardly spoke to me in the two days before they went. I watched them leave in a taxi. *I'm not*

what he wants, I thought over and over.

He never talked to me about Mowgli. He didn't believe me about the drama club. He didn't like me any more.

I sat at the piano with my hands resting on the smooth cool lid.

Would Dad miss me? I'd never wondered that before.

Irena came and found me. "Your dad is sad because you don't want to go with him," she said. "And Vanessa said to look on your bed."

I ran upstairs. Across the bed lay my tailcoat – it was finished. Vanessa had shaped the tails into perfect 'V's and sewn round the edges. And she'd neatened the collar. I held the coat against me. A note was pinned to it.

For Lucas, looking forward to seeing you wearing this when I'm home. V

✗

That evening I watched a film with Irena. I discovered she liked eating sweets in the scary bits. It was a film about zombies with a lot of shocks, so we got through a lot of sweets. We played table tennis too. She was really good, but she didn't shout out her score like Dad sometimes did; she just played fast.

"I play often with my cousins," she said, leaping after the ball and smashing it over the net.

"How many cousins do you have?" I asked.

"Twelve."

I laughed. "Oh. No wonder you're good at it."

There was a lot to do to get ready for the show. Sometimes, in the morning, Keely and I painted or made things. The well had buckets of paper flowers and decorations and we'd made a cobbled street and the fronts of the shops and village houses. It looked amazing. All the costumes were ready too. In the first rehearsal in costume no one got their lines right because they were too busy admiring each other.

I knew how long the talking bits lasted, and, if a bit was slow I could add twiddly bits or play faster to catch up. We put up posters in the café and down the high street to persuade people to come. Avalon said if we had a good audience, we could get donations in buckets. "This hut is not worthy of you all," she said. "You're such a talented bunch."

I practised sitting down in my jacket, flicking

back the tails and playing to the empty ballroom. I tried rolling in on rollerblades but I couldn't press the piano pedals if I wore them.

✗

The weather continued, boiling hot, and the café sold out of ice creams every day. Keely and I helped Jim carry back stacks of ice creams from the wholesaler's.

I spoke to Dad and Vanessa. On the screen they looked very smart, ready to go out for dinner. "How are you?" Dad asked, then straight away: "Is it still hot?"

"Yes," I said.

I thanked Vanessa for sewing my tailcoat.

"It's hot here too... Are you wearing that coat for a performance at the end?" she asked.

"Yes. There is ... something."

"Well, good luck with it. Break a leg, isn't that what they say?"

Chapter 36
Shouting

The rain began early the next morning. It was strange to stare out of the window at pouring rain. The summer had been so dry and baking I'd forgotten what it was like.

Keely and Robbie appeared after breakfast in raincoats. She pulled off Robbie's wellies and her wet trainers. She had her rollerblades over her shoulder.

"Come to the ballroom. I've got something to show you," I said.

Irena scooped Robbie into her arms and we all ran upstairs. I rushed to my room to collect my rollerblades, put them on outside the door and glided in.

"Told you you'd learn it," Keely said as we set off together across the floor.

I turned a full circle with my arms out.

"Did you practise for a long time?" she asked.

"Yes."

"You're quite good now."

We did some loops of the ballroom while Irena made a fuss of Robbie, then we both tried on our costumes for the show.

That afternoon, in the final rehearsal, everyone

was collecting props and practising their opening positions in costume. I was saving my tailcoat for the performance.

"Let's make a start," Avalon shouted over all the excited voices.

I was already at the piano, improvising the first tune while everyone was getting in place. I looked up at the cobwebby roof and the light dancing in the cracks. The hut went darker as the rain streaked down the windows. Avalon switched the lights on. We seemed closed inside, like a ship in a storm.

Something made me look up again and I stopped playing. A kind of ripple ran right across the roof of the hut. A bit of dust flaked down. I could hear the rain drumming, but another sound too, a sort of cracking.

"Listen," I said.

Nobody heard. The cracking sound continued but there were too many chatting voices.

"All of you, *shut up*!" I shouted.

The whole hut went silent; everyone froze in surprise.

"Listen!"

More flakes of plaster floated down. The

splitting sound was getting louder.

My voice rose. "It's the roof. I think we need to…"

My eyes met Avalon's and we both looked up. There was a low creaking from behind me.

"Get out. All of you. Run!" Avalon shouted. "Leave everything!"

I leaped from my seat and sped down the hut. Everyone was moving: people fell, jostled, trailing bits of costumes, out into the rain.

"Move!" Avalon roared from behind us. "Run!"

People grabbed on to each other, falling through the doorway. We skidded across the dead grass all the way to the fence, turned and looked back through the rain.

Crunch.

As we watched, the back wall of the hut crumbled and collapsed, and the whole roof wobbled, tilted and broke apart.

Whoosh.

Dust puffed out in a cloud from underneath. The piano must be crushed inside.

It was like watching a film: everyone had wide-open horrified mouths.

"Are you all here?" Avalon screamed.

"Yes!" we all called.

We counted, counted again.

We were a crowd of wet people in bits of clothes and costumes. I tried to understand what had happened.

Avalon made phone calls. "Police... Yes, this is an emergency."

"My phone's inside on the windowsill," Connie said, her voice trembling.

Someone else said, "My costume's in there on the floor."

"My shoes are inside," Keely said.

I looked at everyone's feet; most people had bare feet and stood in puddles on the dead grass. I still had my trainers on.

"No one goes near that hut," Avalon thundered. She put a shaking hand to her mouth. "Promise me."

We nodded silently.

Rain dripped off my nose. I took off my red baseball cap, squeezed it out and put it on again.

Alan said, "Lucas just saved all our lives, like completely."

"He did," Keely said. "I didn't know you could shout that loud, Lucas."

"Neither did I," I said.

Chapter 37
The Offer

Sirens sounded and we all sat on the wall and watched the hut. The police arrived and checked names. The rain turned to drizzle. Still we stared at the hut. It was as if we thought a new terrible thing might happen, and we had to keep checking. Avalon ticked off a list as each person was collected. Two police put orange tape round the doorway so no one would go near it.

Keely leaped on and off the wall in her muddy bare feet. "How did you know, Lucas?" she asked. "We could all be dead."

"I saw the roof wobble," I told her. "I heard something in the wall."

"And you shouted *get out*."

"I think I just shouted *shut up*. It was Avalon who shouted *get out*."

I texted Irena. *Please meet me at the café. We finished early.*

Gran appeared and swept me into a hug. "Thank goodness. Thank goodness!" she kept saying. "What a mess. You were all so lucky."

"Yes, Gran," Keely said. "How did you know to come and get me?"

"Avalon rang," Gran said.

The last of the kids went home, Avalon finished

talking to the police and they locked up the gate and put signs on it warning people to stay away. "Come and join us, Lucas," Gran said. "Don't go home on your own. The stragglers are coming to Bakewell."

Avalon was on her phone, marching ahead of us up the street.

"Lucas is psychic, Gran," Keely said as she hopped along the pavement.

Gran passed her phone to Keely. "Talk to your mum, will you? She says she wants to hear your voice."

Keely took the phone. "Hi, Mum... Yes ... no, we're all fine..."

As we walked I realised something terrible. It filled my head with a kind of panic.

"Lucas knew... I think he might be telepathic..." Keely said into the phone.

My insides twisted. Of course ... my wish! Now I'd thought of it I couldn't think of anything else. I had to tell someone. I couldn't bear it. "Gran," I said, "when we started the club and we had to choose a wish..."

Gran nodded and smiled at me.

"Well, I wished the hut would fall down ...

because I didn't want to be in the club … and now, well…"

Gran laughed. "Look, love, if all my wishes had come true over the years some really terrible things would have happened. Come here." She hugged me. "Sounds to me like you were a bit of a hero back there, shouting to everyone to get out."

I blushed. "I was loud," I said.

"You know, it's what we *do* that counts. You do know that, don't you? Everyone thinks bad things from time to time." She mock-punched me. "You live too much in that head of yours," she said.

Keely was still jabbering away on the phone. "No, and guess what? My shoes are still inside… I won't tread in any dog poo… Lots of people left their shoes… Because I never wear them… Because it's hot. I don't know. At least I'm alive!"

We went into the café. Keely's mum came out and hugged her. Keely's dad appeared from the kitchen, drying his hands on his apron, hugged Keely too, and pulled up a chair. "So sorry to hear this," I heard him say. "What a mess."

Avalon flopped down at the table and went on tapping numbers into her phone and talking.

Someone put coffee in front of her and she took big gulps.

Gran took Robbie on her knee and fed him a scone. I seemed to be hungry too and we ate scones and drank lemonade while the adults talked in hushed voices.

There was an odd, sad calm feeling. I kept remembering the *whoosh* sound of the wall and watching it crumble.

After some phone calls, Avalon looked up. "The whole hut's unsafe, they're saying." She laughed bitterly. "That's not a surprise. Until they rebuild it, we can't be in there."

"How long?" Gran asked.

"Weeks. And that's only if the council agree to the repairs."

Avalon looked wrecked. She seemed so flat and sad. "I just can't see a way to put the show on. We'll have to cancel it. I've tried everyone I know. I've tried the scout hut, but that's having repairs too, and the schools are all closed for the summer. This really is a tragedy. And without a venue we can't raise money. How can we get the hut in a better state?"

She thumped the table, making the glasses jump.

"Everything we've worked for is disappearing," she said. "I'll have to let all the families know. I am so, so sorry. I'll go on trying venues, but I'm not optimistic; not with two days to go."

Gran ran her hands through her hair, then waved at the café. "What if we cleared all the tables out of here?"

Keely's mum shook her head. "And put them where? And where do we put the customers?"

I felt cold then hot. There would be no performance. I thought about my red tailcoat and all the hours we had spent rehearsing.

"Have it in the ballroom," I said to Avalon.

"What ballroom? What are you talking about, Lucas?"

"I've got a ballroom. We should do the show in there."

"Lucas, are you serious?" Lots of different moods passed across Avalon's face. "Who should I call?"

"There's only me there and our au pair. My dad's away."

She picked up her phone. "We'd need his permission...?"

"He won't mind. He's pleased I'm doing the

drama. He left Irena in charge. I can check with her."

"Lucas, are you sure about this?"

A kind of terror rose in me now, but I still nodded.

"I've been in his ballroom," Keely announced. "There's chairs for the audience. It'll be great. It's bigger than the hut. And he's got a piano."

Next thing Avalon was on her feet and hugging me. "This is unbelievable," she said.

When I told her, Irena frowned and shook her head.

"It's me that said yes," I said. "I won't let Dad sack you, I promise. It's better if we just do it and don't ask first."

"But…"

"It will make him worry if we tell him. Everything will be normal when he comes home."

Chapter 38
This Way

Next morning I opened the gates for Avalon and watched her striding up the drive. She stood open-mouthed on the step then said a very rude word. "Lucas ... wow ... great ... OK, shoes off, I think."

I showed her upstairs to the ballroom. She turned in circles just the way Keely had the first time she came. "Lucas, this space is perfect," she said. She seemed so happy to be there. "Is this your piano?" she asked, sinking down on to the stool. "Fantastic!"

I pointed out the gold chairs for the audience. I could tell she was having a lot of thoughts. "Mats from the hut," she muttered. "Small children along the front."

She had a cup of coffee in the kitchen and chatted to Irena. "Thanks so much for all your help," she said. "And your dad is ... where, Lucas?"

"He's in Tenerife. On holiday," I said.

Three workmen from the council had rescued the well, some costumes and lots of village things and brought them round. I unrolled the bunting Keely and I had made with the sewing machine. We mended a gash in the side of the well. Avalon sent messages to the other children telling them to bring props and anything that might look good in the village and to come with packed lunches the next day.

She asked me to switch on the fountain before she left. "I just want to see what it does," she said.

There are four dolphins with wide-open mouths and jets of water spurt out into a massive clam shell in the middle. The water sprayed in huge arcs and Avalon roared with laughter. She plunged her arm in. Her sleeve was soaked but she didn't seem to care. "Lucas, have you ever paddled in here?" she asked, swishing her arm around.

"No," I said. "I don't think my dad would like that."

"Of course," she said and grinned. "It's an amazing house, Lucas. But I think the most amazing thing to come out of it is you."

That evening, in the ballroom, I walked round the well while Tiger jumped in and out of it. I felt excited about tomorrow. I put on my tailcoat and played "We Are a Village" on the piano. Then I turned off the chandeliers and sat in the dark thinking of how much Mowgli would have loved jumping in and out of the well too.

✗

I spent the next morning with Gran, Keely and Irena: bringing cakes, getting teacups and things to put money in, making signs for the toilet and checking costumes.

Gran said, "There's folk in the café who would love to come along. If we're going to raise money, there's no point being picky about the audience."

Irena and her friends handed out flyers and we changed the posters on the high street to tell everyone my address.

I couldn't believe our show was really going to happen.

Everyone from the drama club arrived at lunchtime and ate picnics sitting on the ballroom floor on the mats. If anyone dropped a wrapper, Keely shoved a bin bag in their face. She bossed everyone, calling, "There's a toilet down there. Put that in the kitchen," and "No one's allowed to touch the piano!"

"Is this really your house? Do you actually live here?" Connie asked me. "I thought this was just a place Avalon found."

"If it was haunted that would be so cool. Are there any locked rooms ... or bats?" Alan asked.

"No," I said.

He shrugged. "Well, it would be good for ghost stories."

"Can we do drama club here every week?" Teo asked.

"Are your mum and dad celebrities?" Connie asked.

"No."

Gran had set up in the kitchen. "We're selling refreshments afterwards. It's the best way to make money," she said. "There's ice creams in the freezer, soft drinks and cakes."

Irena carefully shut Tiger in Dad's study just before the audience arrived. They flooded noisily up the stairs, following the THIS WAY signs.

We stood at the back of the ballroom, waiting to come on.

"Are you terrified?" Keely asked me.

"Yes," I said.

"That's a good thing," she called, dashing away to hide inside the well.

Avalon was all in black with a huge silver lizard necklace. She waited while the audience piled in, talking and pointing at the pictures and chandeliers. There were at least eighty people.

When she stood up the whole ballroom went quiet. She was that kind of person.

"Good afternoon, everyone. I want to thank Lucas and his family for their amazing offer of this place in our hour of need. We are hugely grateful."

I blushed and felt odd. I didn't really have a family, not a proper one. Only Dad.

"There's refreshments in the kitchen at the end of the show. All donations will go towards repairs to our drama hut. I am super proud of this group of young people. Without further ado we would like to present this summer's show, *The Well of a Thousand Wishes*."

It was time. I imagined Keely crouched inside the well, waiting for her signal. I nodded to Teo and Connie and set off down the middle of the audience. I flicked my tails back and sat down at my dark gleaming piano. My fingers hovered just for a moment as I caught sight of Robbie wriggling at the front on the mats with Keely's mum holding him.

I played "We Are a Village".

The actors all stood in a horseshoe to introduce themselves.

"I'm the newsagent," Becky said. "I wished for an extra arm for stacking the shelves." She waved her extendable fake arm at the audience and they laughed.

"I'm the teacher," Connie said. "I wished for eyes in the back of my head; that way I can see if my class are messing around." She turned so the audience could see the eyeballs on springs on the back of her head.

"I play football for the village club," Alan called. "Now I've got this supercharged football foot." He pretended to do a huge kick. "When I kick the ball it soars the whole way across the pitch, over the stands and out of the football ground."

I dived down into the bustling village world of busy people and my fingers found the notes like old friends. I half closed my eyes, knowing all the tunes by heart.

Keely, the well spirit, was clambering out and the audience were gasping and laughing when all at once a noise sounded, louder than everything. I looked out into the audience. "What on earth is going on?" a familiar voice was demanding crossly.

Dad.

Chapter 39
The Show Must
Go On

Shushing sounded from the audience. Heads turned. Dad had arrived at the back in a red and green summer holiday shirt with a bag slung over one shoulder. My eyes met his across the crowded space. He seemed to blink. I saw his lips, mouthing "*Lucas?*"

What would he do? Would he be very rude? Or wreck something? Or throw us all out?

My heart thudded so loud. My fingers shook. There was a murmur of talking in the audience and I saw Gran at the back darting over to speak to Vanessa.

My palms sweated. I stared at Dad. His mouth was wide open. He was gazing at all the people.

"Lucas!" Teo, waiting for his cue, nodded desperately from the stage.

Avalon came to the front with her hand up for silence.

"We're very lucky that Lucas's father has managed to make it back in time for the show." She waved at all the actors. "I hope the audience won't mind if we start again. Everyone off the stage."

More chairs clattered down.

Avalon nodded to me as if this was normal. "*The Well of a Thousand Wishes.* Take it away,

Lucas."

I nodded back.

The ballroom went quiet. Everyone was waiting for the music. I knew where Dad was, but I didn't look there.

I put my hands on the piano keys again and the music began to flow out of me. The first scene started. All the villagers introduced themselves and told the audience about the well and all the wishes they'd made. Sammy plotted and schemed and everyone booed. During the villain music I noticed Robbie clinging to his mum's legs.

Keely leaped out of the well and talked to the villagers and they decided to send her on holiday.

Soon we were celebrating the villain running away and it was the last chorus of *"We Are a Village"*. I sang along with the others and there was wonderful quiet after my final chords, followed by clapping and cheering. Then we all bowed. The cheering didn't stop.

I looked up and saw Vanessa on a chair near the stage grinning back at me and clapping hard. But there was no sign of Dad, just his empty chair beside her. A huge sad feeling crashed over me; maybe Dad had walked out…

It was over.

I got caught in a crowd of stampeding, celebrating children with Teo, Alan and Keely beside me as we all flooded downstairs for tea.

My head was spinning.

In the kitchen, Gran hugged me. "You are a star, my lovely."

The audience spilled out into the hall and someone put a cake in my hand.

I scoured the kitchen for Dad in his holiday shirt, but he wasn't anywhere. I searched among the people saying well done and eating and drinking and laughing.

I had to find Dad. Why hadn't he stayed to make sure nobody dropped anything on the fossil tiles in the kitchen?

Avalon appeared beside me. And there was Vanessa. "This young man has been amazing. You must be so proud. But then we knew the minute we heard him play."

"We are," Vanessa said.

"Lucas offered your ballroom because we were so stuck," Avalon said. "Otherwise our show would have been cancelled."

"I can see lots of work has gone into this,"

Vanessa said. "The set's amazing. Did you help make everything, Lucas?"

"Yes." I said. "I used the sewing machine."

Keely grabbed my arm, whispering, "Is that your dad's girlfriend?"

"Yeah."

"So is your dad here? Is he cross we used the ballroom?" She frowned. "We didn't make any mess."

"I don't know where he is," I said. "He's gone. Maybe he got a phone call."

"Did he like the show? He must have. He clapped a lot."

"Did he?" I wished I knew.

"Excuse me a minute." Gran grabbed a tray of cakes. "I need to sell this lot." She called to the crowd. "If you enjoy the refreshments, come to Bakewell. We are open every day."

I got away and ran out into the hall. I threw open the doors of each downstairs room.

Dad couldn't have gone out, could he?

Maybe he had got in a car and driven away?

I went upstairs. There would be no one in the ballroom now, just the well standing under the Avalanche chandelier. I glanced inside ... froze.

Someone was in there.

Chapter 40
Wrapped Up

Dad was sitting alone at the piano. My breath stopped. I crossed the wide gleaming floor. Was he so angry he couldn't even speak to me?

"Dad," I said quietly.

He saw me. "Lucas!" Dad's face was streaming with tears. He held out his arms and gathered me into a hug that pulled my legs off the ground until I was on the piano stool beside him. He gripped me so tight. I found I was crying too.

He spoke in a terrible, fierce voice right beside my ear. "You didn't tell me that you could play like that."

"I'm sorry, Dad." I pulled away. "I should have asked permission. But we didn't have anywhere to do the show and we'd been practising for weeks and…" I ran out of words.

He grabbed me again. "Don't be sorry. Your playing is fantastic, Lucas. It's special. Mum would have loved it. It was like – like having her back!" He burst into violent sobs and buried me in the hug again.

It felt so wrong for Dad to cry, like something big breaking apart that should stay safe and whole. Like the Avalanche falling. But he wasn't pushing me away.

"So ... you're not cross?" I asked.

"Why would I be cross? I'm just ... so proud of you." He stared at me as if he didn't recognise me. "You miss Mum. I know. I knew. When she died ... it was just too much ... the way it happened... I just couldn't talk about it... I just had to find a way to ... go on without her."

I felt the hug hard round me, Dad's warm hug. There were so many things I'd wanted to tell Dad and now he seemed like he really wanted to listen.

"I wish I'd said goodbye to her," I said. "I never said goodbye."

His face shook. He pulled back, gripping my arms. His mouth wobbled. "Neither did I!"

"But you were at the hospital."

"Lucas, she didn't wake up. It was so quick."

"You didn't tell me anything. You didn't talk to me."

"You're right. I should have... I'm sorry." He hugged me again. "I just couldn't. I'm so sorry!"

I pulled away again a tiny bit. "Dad. Did Mum play her own made-up tunes like I do?"

His face lit up. "Yes. For herself. I was always finding her making up songs, trying out little phrases and ideas... She wouldn't have played for an audience like you just did, but … yes … she needed it. You're so like her."

"I love it," I said.

"Come here!" Dad held me close.

We stayed there. The hug didn't stop. He didn't want to let me go.

"Dad," I said after a while, "I really can't breathe!"

His arms relaxed. "No, no, good idea. Sorry. Sorry."

We laughed.

We sat side by side. "Lucas, I should have listened," he said. "I've been too wrapped up … work and… Look, it doesn't matter now. What a pair we are. I want to ask you more. Tell me about it later, but, first, let's go down and say hello properly to all these people."

Chapter 41
Ballroom

Evening came. We sat in the ballroom after everyone had gone home except a few people still chatting in the kitchen. I let Tiger out and he played with the bunting. "Dad said he wanted to see your show, so we came home a couple of days early," Vanessa told me.

Dad was smiling. "The show was amazing. This is the reason you didn't want to come on holiday?"

"Yes."

He nodded. "No wonder. You were trying to tell me."

Most of the set had been carefully piled by the doors but the well still stood in the middle.

"We can move it all tomorrow," Dad said.

My phone beeped, beeped again.

I checked my messages. "Can I have some friends round tomorrow from drama club?"

Dad smiled. "Of course you can."

"Can I join again, next term?"

Dad nodded. "Absolutely!"

I looked up into the Avalanche, hanging over the well. A huge tired relief filled me.

Vanessa smiled. "You looked brilliant in the jacket, Lucas."

"Thanks," I said, looking from Vanessa to Dad and back to Vanessa.

Dad definitely looked different. Maybe it was all the smiling.

I grinned back at Dad. "I can rollerblade now too," I said. "Do you want to see?"

I ran to get Keely from the kitchen.

Together we skated around the ballroom. Sometimes we glided all the way down and turned, smoothly looping, powering back across the floor, meeting in the middle, waving and laughing.

I caught glimpses: Robbie sitting with Dad and Tiger, Vanessa taking Robbie over to the windows, Robbie following Tiger, Dad standing by the windows talking to Gran. I met Keely in the middle and we skated round the well. Always there was music in my head: "We Are a Village" in long curves and spirals.

I glided over and played piano for Keely to skate to. I played all my favourite tunes from the show and Dad came to sit beside me on the stool again. We watched Keely turning and grinning and her arms were stretched out then pressed close to her chest.

A long time ago big dances must have happened here. Everyone must have dressed like me in tailcoats or like Keely in her floating purple ribbons and Christmas decoration hat. People danced and made music. And just for that evening in the spinning world, time stopped, and I knew Mum was with me, holding Mowgli, just smiling from somewhere in the walls and enjoying the lights from the chandeliers, the skating and laughing and the sound of her piano playing in the ballroom.

Acknowledgements

I'd like to thank the Howes, the Briggses, my friends, writing friends and the staff and children in the schools where I work for their brilliant continued support.

Huge thanks to Tom Bonnick, my editor and Anne Clark my agent, both special people who understand and support my writing.

Thanks to all at the amazing Nosy Crow for all you do to make books fly.

How to be Me springs from my love of music. My parents, and especially my dad, understood how important playing the piano was for me when I was growing up. Despite taking lessons, I soon preferred to play just for myself, improvising around tunes and finding my own accompaniments. My dad would let me get down from the table after a family meal and 'practise' instead of helping to clear up because it made him happy to hear me play. Playing the piano still transforms my mood and music remains a key part of who I am.

All the creative arts have a special kind of power; they can unlock something inside us and help us discover who we are. I think teachers of creative subjects are often unsung heroes, helping children to thrive.